... be returned on or before
... below

Oxford University Press
Oxford

Jacqueline Wilson

# Nobody's Perfect

*with an afterword by the author*

**Oxford University Press**
*Oxford  Toronto  Melbourne*

Oxford University Press, Walton Street, Oxford OX2 6DP

*Oxford New York Toronto*
*Delhi Bombay Calcutta Madras Karachi*
*Petaling Jaya Singapore Hong Kong Tokyo*
*Nairobi Dar es Salaam Cape Town*
*Melbourne Auckland*

and associated companies in
*Beirut Berlin Ibadan Nicosia*

*Oxford* is a trade mark of Oxford University Press

First published 1982
First published in this edition 1987

© Jacqueline Wilson 1982
Author's afterword © Jacqueline Wilson 1987

ISBN 0 19 2715763

Printed in Great Britain

# *Chapter 1*

*I* WROTE my name and address in the right-hand corner of yet another piece of notepaper and sighed. I'd woken up with an idea for the writing competition and I'd been nursing it in my head all morning while we struggled round Sainsburys. It was going to be a stark and sordid story. I hoped the judges would be shocked and impressed. My fifteen-year-old heroine – Miranda? Cressida? Pandora? – was going to run away from her coarse, cruel stepfather and indifferent mother. She would roam London, living in assorted squalid squats, then fall in love with a drug addict, a lean, dark-eyed, wild-haired poet, and they would have a passionate affair before his tragic death from an overdose.

I liked this part the most. I slid into a day-dream about the poet – Joss? Tristram? Laurence? – whilst I flicked the discarded balls of paper up and down the table with my pen nib.

'Sandra! What a waste of paper. And you'll get ink on that good teak if you're not careful.'

I sighed again, parted from my dream poet just as he was tenderly caressing my white breasts. Well, not *my* breasts, of course. They are not worth caressing, still barely needing their 32" small cup Marks and Sparks natural look bra.

'What are you doing anyway? Is that homework?' said Mum suspiciously, taking the table-cloth out of the sideboard.

'Sort of. English.'

'I thought it was Maths and French at the week-end,' Mum said, rattling in the cutlery drawer. Her hand suddenly shot out and seized one of the crumpled pieces of paper.

'Don't look!' I snatched it back.

'Don't be so rude.'

'Well, it's private.'

'What is it? Here, you're not going in for that writing competition that was in the paper the other day?'

'No.'

'Oh Sandra, do you have to be so secretive? Go in for it if you want to, love. Only don't be too disappointed if you don't get anywhere. They have thousands entering for that sort of thing. Anyway, hurry up. You'll have to come off that table in five minutes. Stan and Julie will be back in a tick.'

She went into the kitchen, humming, beating time on her hip with the teaspoons.

'Great. She only expects me to write a literary masterpiece in five rotten minutes,' I muttered.

'What?' Mum called from the kitchen.

'Nothing.'

I started my story for the sixth time.

'Miranda pulled on her clothes, slung her bag over her shoulder, and crept downstairs. She closed the front door behind her and took a great gulp of the early morning air. Freedom!'

I read it through, thought for a moment, and then changed Miranda to Pandora. I read it through again, decided it was a little sparse, and scribbled several hasty insertions.

I ended up with: 'Cressida pulled on her stripy Osh Kosh dungarees, slung her handmade carpet-bag over her shoulders, and crept stealthily downstairs in her red and navy suede Kickers.'

It was beginning to sound more like a fashion page than a serious story. I sighed and crumpled that piece of paper too. I was only using school file paper so it didn't really matter. I wrote my name yet again on a fresh sheet of paper and frowned. Sandra Smith. Of all the names in the whole world, how could Mum have deliberately chosen Sandra?

'My best friend at school was called Sandra. She had lovely long blonde hair and she was allowed to wear stiletto heels long before the rest of us. I'd have given anything to

2

swop places with Sandra,' Mum once said, when I asked her. 'I think it's a nice name.'

'But it's so ordinary.'

'Well, so what?' said Mum.

I was determined to be as extraordinary as possible. Winning this writing competition was only the beginning. I've wanted to be a writer ever since I was little. I've made up stories in my head for as long as I can remember. It's the writing it all down on paper that's the difficult part.

My competition story had seemed marvellous while I was still making it up but down on paper it seemed silly and childish. Perhaps Mum was right and I didn't stand a chance of winning.

'Are you off that table yet, Sandra? Lay it for me, there's a love.'

I hadn't got very far. I wrote my name a second time, in fancy copperplate, and then I had a go at italics, but Sandra Smith still didn't look at all literary. I tried hard to visualise a whole row of Sandra Smith novels on the library shelf but it wasn't easy. Then I thought of all the contemporary women writers I'd heard of and I cheered up. Their Mums hadn't gone in for stylish names either. Margaret and Beryl and Edna, Doris and Iris and Muriel. They sounded more like charladies in flowery pinnies and pompom slippers than serious novelists.

I heard the key in the front door and then Julie's excited babbling.

'Hello, my little lovie. Have a nice dance? Did you ask Miss Miles about the cat costume, Stan? I haven't got a clue how to do the headpiece. Oh Sandra!' Mum came in from the hall, arms folded, her chin drawn in. 'You really are the limit, Sandra.'

No wonder I dislike my name. Mum is forever reproaching me with it.

'Sorry.' I gathered up my bits and threw the table-cloth over the good teak. Mum is very proud of the dining suite Stan bought when they were first married. When there was just Mum and me and we lived in two rooms we had a scratched teak veneer table and a teak veneer sideboard with

3

silly wobbling legs. I can't say I think much of any sort of teak, good or cheap veneer. When I branch out on my own I shall live in an airy Victorian attic and I shall have sensible scrubbed pine.

I often design my dream flat and all its furniture and imagine myself living there. I'd quite like to have boy-friends – well, lovers – but I shall live alone.

Julie came skipping into the living-room and started doing her cat dance, her anorak half on, half off.

'Look at me, Sandra. Look at me doing my pussy dance.'

'No thanks.'

'Mum, Miss Miles says please can I have whiskers, be-cause she wants me to twirl them,' Julie said, doing bunny hops across the carpet.

'Watch out, Julie. You look more like a rabbit than a cat,' I snapped.

'Out the way, pet,' said Stan, snatching her up and twirling her round. 'You did have a nice dance today, didn't you? Light as a little fairy, eh?'

'How does she expect me to make whiskers? Look, it takes me all my time to sew a button on, how can I make a proper cat costume? Is that table laid yet, Sandra, I'm dishing up.'

'Pipe cleaners.'

'What did you say, Sandra?'

'Pipe cleaners,' I repeated patiently, dealing out the table mats.

'What are you talking about?'

Mum brought in two plates of individual chicken pie, peas and chips, and went back for two more. Stan opened a large bottle of Tizer and splashed it into the tumblers. He held his out to Julie.

'Through the teeth, round the gums, look out stomach, here it comes,' he said, swallowing fizz. I didn't think it funny the first time I heard him say it. I've lost track of how many times he's said it since. But Julie giggled. Five is the right age for appreciating Stan's humour.

'What was that you were muttering when I was out in the kitchen?' said Mum, tucking into her chicken pie.

'Pipe rotten cleaners. Are you deaf or stupid?'

It sounded ruder than I'd intended. I was about to say sorry, but Stan exploded before I had a chance.

'Don't you dare talk to your mother like that! I've had just about enough of your madamish ways. You apologise.'

'Stan!'

'No, Mary, she's got to be told. Come on, Sandra. It's time you learnt to toe the line. Say you're sorry.'

My blood pumped round my body at an alarming rate. I could feel myself going bright red as they all stared at me. I couldn't say a word.

'Apologise this instant!' Stan was very red too. His big ears were a luminous scarlet. I stared at his ears, hating him. He has a terrible habit of poking his little finger in his ear and waggling it vigorously. I imagined him doing it now, so that I wouldn't be frightened. He'd never once hit me but I knew he sometimes wanted to.

'And take that insolent expression off your face too! Are you going to apologise?' Stan's voice rose to a roar. Julie started fidgeting, lifting the skirt of her dress and nuzzling into it, as if it was her old cuddle nappy.

'Look at you, you've upset your little sister now,' Stan blustered. 'Apologise or leave the table.'

I stood up. The backs of my knees were wet. I turned and walked slowly towards the door, determined not to look upset.

'Oh Sandra, come back. Don't be silly,' said Mum. 'Her lunch will get cold, Stan.'

'Serve her right.'

I walked on, out of the door and upstairs to my bedroom. I sat on the edge of my bed, shivering, although I was so hot. My throat felt tight, as if I was going to cry, but I was determined not to give Stan the satisfaction. I didn't care about missing lunch anyway. I'm not very keen on Mum's sort of food. She had to rely on convenience food when she went out to work full time, and now it's become a habit. When I have my own place I shall have natural organic food. There's a lovely new wholefood shop opened up down the road, and I persuaded Mum to buy some stuff there, but Stan had a moan.

5

'What do we want with all these odd bean things? They give me wind. And I had enough of lentils and split peas when I was a kid. It seems daft buying this muck when we can afford a nice bit of steak or whathaveyou.'

Stan is forever harping on about his deprived childhood, when his bum-hung-out-of-his-breeches. He was one of seven kids and his Dad drank. Well, at least he had a Dad. I had a deprived childhood too. Damp furnished rooms and child-minders, day nurseries and ten weeks in Care.

I found I was crying in spite of myself. If I'm really honest I have to admit that I can't remember all that much about those early tooing and froing days.

I can remember being in Care though. Mum had a nervous breakdown and wouldn't get up for days. I was five, Julie's age, and yet I made Mum cups of tea and went down to the local shop with Mum's purse and got myself to school and back. I managed for quite a while, until a teacher noticed something was up. I thought Mum was dying and when they took me away to the Children's Home I was sure I'd never see her again.

They made me eat fatty bacon for breakfast my first morning and I was sick into my mug of hot sugared milk. I was so scared of wetting the bed at night that I kept getting up every couple of hours to run to the lavatory. The girl in the bed next to me always wet herself and she got smacked. I wasn't smacked the whole time I was there. The House-mother was quite kind to me. She once took me on her lap and cuddled me but she clasped me so tightly round the stomach I felt sick again. I still sometimes dream I'm back in the Home and wake up with a sour ache in my stomach because I'm so scared.

I was still crying for that little five-year-old Sandra when Mum came in with my chicken pie on a tray.

'Oh love.' She put the tray down and sat beside me.

'I said pipe cleaners,' I sobbed. 'They'd make good cat's whiskers for Julie's costume.'

'So they would.' Mum put her arm round me, snuggling my head into her shoulder. 'You silly old sausage,' she said, rocking me, as if I really had shrunk back to five again. 'Stan didn't really mean to upset you, pet. Come on now, dry those eyes.'

I let her go on thinking I was crying because Stan had shouted at me. By the time I'd calmed down the chicken pie was cold and I'd gone off it anyway, so Mum made me a toasted cheese sandwich. I came downstairs to eat it. Stan was in the kitchen, getting on with the washing-up to make amends. We nodded at each other in an embarrassed way and that was that. I didn't ever actually apologise.

I made a fresh start on my story while I nibbled my sandwich. Julie came begging for a bite and tried to read what I was doing.

'It's all squiggles, your writing, Sandra. Read it to me.'

'No. It's private. Oh do buzz off, Julie.'

'Sandra's writing a story, pet,' said Mum.

'I want to write a story too,' said Julie, sitting up at the table with me.

'Give her a bit of paper to keep her quiet, there's a good girl,' Mum said to me.

I sighed irritably, but I didn't feel like starting another row so I gave Julie one piece of paper and an old felt-tip pen. She laid her hand flat on the paper and drew round it carefully with the pen. That's about all she's learnt to do at school so far. She looked at her wobbly blue hand with satisfaction.

'Look Mum. Look Dad. Look at my drawing.'

There was a chorus of approval for the infant Dürer.

'Now I'm going to write my story,' she announced. 'What's your story about, Sandra?'

'I told you, it's private. It's too grown-up for you, anyway.'

'Write about the three bears, Julie,' Mum suggested.

'No. That story's in my book. I want to write my own story.'

'Write a story about a little girl ballet dancer,' said Stan.

Julie wrinkled her nose.

'What's your story *about*, Sandra?'

'Oh God. A girl.'

'A little girl?'

'No, a big one.'

'Like you?'

'Yes.'

'Is it about you then?'

'It could be.'

'I'll write about you too. And me. And all of us.'

She looked at her drawing and then turned the page over. 'I'll write about our hands to go with my picture.'

'Oh, Julie, you are a funny kid,' said Mum fondly.

I did my best to ignore both of them and wrote for more than an hour. The story was going well now. Rosamund – I seemed to have rechristened her quite a lot – had weathered her love affair with the drug addict poet and walked tearfully away from his grave, older and wiser by far. But I didn't know what to do with her then. I didn't want her to trail back home. That would be such an anti-climax. But I didn't want her to carry on wandering either. I wanted to finish the story by having her striding out purposefully in her Kickers to . . . ?

# *Chapter 2*

*I* DECIDED to leave my story for the moment. Stan had 'Grandstand' blaring on the telly and it was hard to concentrate. Julie had scribbled a few sentences, drawn five or six further hands, and was now sitting on Stan's lap sucking a Curly Wurly. Glistening strands of toffee scarred her cheeks. She'd made a sticky patch on Stan's forehead too but he didn't seem to mind.

He was tucking into a box of Maltesers, throwing them one by one up in the air and trying to catch them in his mouth. Julie squealed and clapped each time. Mum was eating a bar of Limmits chocolate. She's not as fat as Stan, but she's a good stone overweight and it's a squeeze for her to get into a size fourteen dress now although she used to be as skinny as me.

'You eat diet chocolate instead of meals, not as well as,' I said.

'I'm only having a little nibble,' said Mum, devouring two more squares. 'And I don't think it's as fattening as proper chocolate.'

I raised my eyebrows at her stupidity.

'Your Mum doesn't need to fuss about her weight anyway,' said Stan, reaching over and patting her thigh appreciatively. It was straining the seams of her old fashioned French-cut polyester trousers but this was obviously to Stan's taste. 'Your Mum's got a smashing figure.'

I hated it when he talked like that. I couldn't look at his huge hand or Mum's pleased pink cheeks.

'You're the one who needs fattening up, Sandra,' said the overgrown sea-lion, catching another Malteser in his mouth. 'Have a chocolate.'

'No thanks.'

'There's your pudding still out in the kitchen. You never ate it,' said Mum.

'It was butterscotch Angel Delight, yummy yummy,' said Julie. 'I licked out the mixing bowl, didn't I, Mum? Can I have Sandra's if she doesn't want it?'

'I do want it,' I said quickly, and went out to the kitchen.

I scraped my spoon round the dish several times, not bothering to taste the congealing tan slush and then quickly rinsed it under the tap. Mum followed me out into the kitchen and looked at me reproachfully.

'That was a bit mean.'

'I ate most of it. And besides, you shouldn't let Julie make such a pig of herself. She's getting ever so fat,' I said quickly.

'She's not fat. She's meant to be a bit cuddly, it's her build.'

'Takes after her Daddy, does she?'

'Oh Sandra.'

'Sorry.'

'No, you're not. You have to keep getting at him, don't you?'

'No.'

Mum sighed. 'And I wish you weren't so obsessive about people's weight. It isn't half off-putting, having you glaring at us whenever we have a bit of chocolate or whatever. You'll be getting that slimming disease thing if you're not careful. There was a programme about it the other afternoon while you were at school. It's got me all worried now. I forget what you call it, something Nervous. . . .'

'Anorexia Nervosa?'

'All right, no need to swank. It's an awful thing, Sandra, some girls actually die of it.'

'Yes, I know. Well, you and Stan had better live in hope then. Maybe I'll vomit up all my meals and waste away to nothing and then all your problems will be solved.'

I'd meant it as a joke but Mum looked shocked.

'That's an awful thing to say.'

'I didn't mean it,' I said irritably, glad that the phone had started ringing so I could get away. 'Shall I answer it?'

It was Kim, wanting to speak to me. I was surprised. We were still technically friends at school, but we hadn't been close for ages. We used to be best friends and phoned every evening and stayed with each other at week-ends, but when we were split up into different sets everything changed. Kim started to be friends with Debra Hannagan and they went to discos and the Hay Waggon pub with a crowd of boys who'd already left school. Kim and Debra look years older than me now, and they think they act it too.

'What are you doing tonight then, Sandra?' Kim asked.

'Oh, nothing much. I might go to Wedgies or perhaps I'll troll around to Tramps.'

'What are you on about?' said Kim, clearly not appreciating my sarcasm. '*Are* you doing anything tonight, Sandra? Because I've got this date all lined up for you if you're free.'

'What?'

'This boy. His name's Roy Johnson and he's ever so nice. You know I'm going out with a boy called Jeff, well, Roy's his mate. We thought we'd all go for a drink somewhere, maybe have a meal out. Roy's dying to meet you, San.'

'How can he be? How does he know anything about me?'

'I've told him, haven't I? Now, we'll pick you up at about half seven, okay?'

'No!'

'Later? Okay, how about eight o'clock?'

'No, I don't want to go!'

'What's going on?' said Mum. 'Is that Kim? What does she want you to do?'

'Oh go on,' said Kim. 'You haven't got a boy-friend, have you, San? You haven't ever had one, have you?'

'Well, so what?'

'So it's about time you got yourself fixed up,' said Kim. 'It'll be a great night out, you'll really enjoy yourself.'

'I don't want to. And anyway, I thought you went round with Debra. Why can't she go out with this Roy?'

'Oh her. I'm getting a bit fed up with her actually. She's a bit cheap, if you ask me. And she's got this other boy she goes with, anyway. No, you come, San, please.'

'Is this a date?' said Mum.

'Aye aye,' said Stan.

'Go, Sandra! Go on, love, be a devil,' Mum urged.

I turned my back on them both.

'Look, we'll be round for you at half-past seven, like I said. You'll take to Roy, really you will. He's a bit shy and serious, like you, so you ought to get on well together.'

'I'm not shy,' I said furiously, blushing with rage.

'All right, all right, keep your hair on. Well look, I've got to rush now, so we'll see you tonight, right? Jeff will have the loan of this car, so we'll be doing things in style. See you, San. 'Bye.'

'No!'

But she'd already hung up. I dialled her number, ignoring Mum's questions, but could only get an engaged tone.

'I didn't even think you were still friendly with Kim,' said Mum. 'Oh I am glad for you, Sandra. It'll do you good to get out and have a bit of fun. It worries me, the way you're stuck in all the time, just sitting with your head in a book. It's time you got to know a few boys.'

'I'm not going.'

'Of course you are. Don't be silly. There's no need to get into a state. Tell us all about this boy then.'

'I don't know a thing about him and I don't want to either.'

'Well, you'll have to ask him in so we can get a good look at him. We can't have you going out with any old Joe Bloggs,' said Mum. 'What about your hair? Would you like me to put it up in rollers for you, give it a bit of bounce?'

'No thanks.' Hair rollers! 'And I keep telling you, I'm not going. I don't want to go out with a complete stranger. He's bound to be awful anyway, or Kim would want him for herself. Obviously Debra's already turned her nose up at him. And why does everyone automatically assume I'm desperate to get myself a boy-friend? I'd probably be bored out of my mind with this Roy person.' I carried on in a similar vein for several minutes, trying to convince someone, even if it was only myself.

'There's no need to be scared, love,' said Mum, with a silly smile on her face. 'You're bound to feel a bit shy at first, but you'll soon get over that.'

'I am not shy. Oh for God's sake, all right, I'll go, just to prove my point. And stop grinning at me, Mum. Look, I'd better go and get some homework done, right?'

I went upstairs to my room and peered in my mirror. There was a spot on my chin and several others lurking beneath my fringe. Perhaps I'd try slapping on a bit of Mum's foundation cream. And I'd better borrow her make-up. I'd had several interesting Biba eye-shadows and lip-sticks but I'd thrown them all away shortly after I started subscribing to *Spare Rib*. I still wanted to be a feminist – but I wanted to look pretty too.

Only I'd never look pretty no matter how I prinked with powder and paint. I was too small and skinny. I looked much younger than fifteen. And I wore glasses too. I liked my little round gold-rimmed glasses very much. I'd had to make do with National Health glasses up till last year. But some boys didn't like girls in any kind of glasses. On the bus on the way home from school some boys were discussing us girls in loud voices, weighing us up.

'I don't reckon that skinny old Four-Eyes,' said one, and they all guffawed.

That was me. But they were only pathetic little school-boys. Roy would probably be older. Kim had said he was shy and serious. I liked that. Perhaps he wore glasses too. I imagined him: thin, sensitive, with soft, straight hair falling in his eyes. Maybe he was at a sixth-form college somewhere, studying. Perhaps he wasn't used to girls. Suppose he'd never even gone out with a girl before. He might be dreading tonight too, wondering what on earth I'd be like and whether he'd be able to think of things to say. But maybe we'd find we had so much in common that we'd both forget to be shy. We'd leave Kim and her boy-friend and go off somewhere by ourselves and walk hand in hand in the moonlight and tell each other all sorts of secrets and then we'd stop and kiss and. . . .

You'd think I subscribed to *Woman's Own* instead of *Spare Rib*.

I knew I was a fool to get all hopeful and excited about Roy but I couldn't help it. I didn't do any homework of course. I didn't even give my competition story another thought. I spent the rest of the afternoon having a bath and washing my hair and trying on practically every single garment in my wardrobe.

'Wear your pretty Laura Ashley dress,' said Mum.

'What, that pink one? Yes, I like that,' said Stan.

'It's too dressy. You don't dress up to go out nowadays,' I said. 'You wear casual clothes. Only I haven't got any decent casual clothes.'

'Well, wear your jeans then.'

'Decent, I said. I can't wear those old jeans, the legs are all cut wrong. They're too old-fashioned for words.'

'You only got them six months ago! And I thought you were the one who despised fashion. You wanted to slummock around in those awful baggy dungarees.'

'I still do. You know I'd give anything to have dungarees. If I had dungarees there wouldn't be any problem. What *am* I going to wear? I can't wear my cords, they're much too hot, and they need cleaning anyway.'

'Wear your party dress, Sandra, your lovely turquoise party dress,' said Julie, referring to a hideous long chiffon creation that Stan gave me two Christmases ago. It was supposed to be floorlength but now it comes inches above my ankles, thank God, so I can't wear it any more.

I ended up wearing my old denim skirt and a green cotton shirt, blue and green striped socks, and my black strap dance shoes.

'I still don't think blue and green go together, love. And I've never been keen on those socks, they look like football strip,' Mum said doubtfully.

'Mary! I think you look smashing, Sandra,' said Stan.

I shuffled awkwardly, not wanting his compliments. I couldn't remember whether Kim had said they'd be round at half-past seven or eight. I kept having to dash to the loo and I felt horribly hot and sweaty, although I'd rubbed half a tube of deodorant under my arms. I hunched my shoulders and stuck out my elbows so that my shirt no longer came in

14

contact with my damp armpits.

'Sandra! Stand up straight. Here, what's that stuff you've got round your eyes?'

I'd done a bit of improvising with a black felt-tip pen. It had smudged a little but I'd hoped it wouldn't show behind my glasses.

Mum came to inspect me and I shied away from her.

'Hold still. My God, you look like a panda.' She licked the corner of her hanky.

'Stop it. Look, it's meant to be like that. Mum!'

Julie giggled excitedly.

'Sandra is a panda! Sandra is a panda! Sandra is a panda!' she chanted tediously.

'Leave her alone, you two,' said Stan. 'You'll drive the poor girl mad. Here, Sandra, stick this in your purse.' He handed me a couple of pound notes. 'If you feel you want to come home at any time you can use this as taxi money. Do you think she'll need any more, Mary? They'll pay for her, won't they? The two boys? Or don't blokes pay for girls any more in these dread days of Women's Lib?'

'Don't ask me,' said Mum. 'Maybe she ought to have a fiver, just in case.'

'Look, they probably won't even turn up. I told Kim I didn't want to come. And I still don't. In fact I don't think I'm going to go even if they do call round for me.'

The doorbell chimed and my heart started thudding.

'Don't answer it!' I said, but Julie was already rushing out into the hall. I wondered about running upstairs to hide in my room but Mum might come and drag me out. I walked into the hall instead. My legs felt limp, like paper. Julie opened the door and yelled, 'It's Kim, it's Kim, she's here.'

'Shut up,' I hissed, and got myself to the door. It was a wonder Julie had recognised Kim. Her hair was dragged up into a high fifties-style pony-tail. She was wearing a low-cut blouse and a tight black skirt with a slit at the side and she seemed taller than ever because she was wearing black suede stilettoes.

I decided she looked like a tart but I couldn't help being impressed. She'd applied her make-up with all the skill I lacked, and she looked very pretty in a cheap sort of way. Not just pretty. Sexy.

'Hi, San,' she said, eyeing me up and down too.

There was a glint in her eye that I didn't like. If she'd had Debra with her I knew they'd have nudged each other and giggled at me. But she didn't seem to have anyone with her.

'Where are they, then?'

'The boys? They're in the car, just round the corner. They couldn't park any nearer. Come on, San. You taking a jacket? I've got a cardi in the car.'

Mum bore down on me. She stared at Kim.

'Good evening, Mrs Smith,' said Kim, smiling sweetly.

'Hello Kim,' said Mum, sounding shocked. 'Goodness, don't you look grown-up. Now, where are these two boys? How about all coming in for a quick coffee?'

'Oh no thanks, we're in a bit of a hurry. Come *on*, San.'

'Wait a minute! Now Kim, what exactly are you doing this evening?'

'Just having a pleasant night out.'

'But where? Are you going to the pictures or a disco or what?'

'Probably. We haven't quite decided yet.'

'Well, I don't like Sandra just going off into the blue. And look Kim, I think you both ought to be back by ten. Well, half past at the latest. That's quite late enough.'

'Don't worry, Mrs Smith, we'll look after San and get her back home safely,' said Kim, as if she were years older than me. She pulled my arm and I found myself walking down the garden path.

'Have a nice time,' Mum called doubtfully.

Kim linked arms with me.

'Doesn't she go on?' she whispered. 'I don't know how you stand it, San. What you got them funny socks on for, eh? Never mind, maybe Roy's kinky about stripy socks, you never know. There they are, look. By the Ford Escort.'

There were two boys leaning against the car lighting cigarettes. One had fair curly hair and a blue suit with terribly sharp creases in the trousers. He had a sharp crease for a nose too, but apart from that he was quite good-looking.

The other boy had dark hair in an ancient teddy-boy style. It was either wet or very greasy. His spots were clearly visible even from right across the street.

I didn't have to ask which one was Roy.

# Chapter 3

*I* WANTED to run away but Kim had hold of my arm.

'Come on, San. Smile!' she hissed, dimpling in Jeff's direction. He grinned back and waggled his finger at her. Roy didn't grin. We stared silently at each other, mutually appalled.

'What are you playing at, Jeff? She's just a kid,' he muttered as we approached.

Jeff and Roy looked much older than us, at least nineteen or twenty. Roy was worse close up. A lot of his spots looked recently squeezed.

'Hello darling,' Jeff said to Kim. 'Great, you've brought along a friend for Roy. Hello sweetheart.'

He directed this second greeting at the infant friend for Roy. I mumbled some kind of reply.

'What's your name then? Sandra? Little Sandy, eh? Well, say hello to Sandy, Roy, make her feel welcome.' Jeff nudged Roy. He looked as if he wanted to run away too. I hoped he would and then I could go straight back home. But he merely nodded at me and winked in a grotesque fashion. At least I think it was a wink. He did it several times, so I didn't dare take any notice, just in case it was an uncontrollable nervous tic.

'Let's go and have a drink then, eh, girls?' said Jeff. 'All pile into the car and off we go.'

Jeff and Kim sat in the front, so I got stuck in the back with Roy. He moved quickly away from me and stared out of the window. I tried to tell myself that I didn't care. I couldn't stand him. But I still minded that he obviously couldn't stand me.

Jeff drove very fast and very badly. He couldn't see much of the road anyway because he had so many mascots suspended from his driving mirror: plush dice, a plastic Smurf, a miniature pair of football boots, an orange hairy animal of indeterminate breed and a turquoise fur fabric dolphin with cross eyes. Jeff treated Kim like a cuddly mascot too, frequently taking his hand off the steering wheel to tickle her under the chin or pinch her cheek. Once he reached over and unmistakably tweaked her nipple. I blushed and pretended not to have noticed. Kim went a bit pink too. But on the whole she seemed to be coping admirably. She giggled and twittered and made cute remarks.

Roy and I said nothing at all. It wasn't long before I began to feel car sick. I usually take a Kwell but I hadn't thought we'd be going so far. I sat very still and stared at the back of Jeff's head while great yellow waves of nausea washed over me. We were now driving along a busy bypass and there wasn't anywhere for Jeff to pull up. I wondered if I was going to have to throw up all over my shirt and skirt and stripy socks.

But mercifully Jeff veered down a side road and then drew up in the car park of a large pub.

'Right, let's go and get tanked up,' he said. 'Soon break the ice, eh, Sandy?'

I smiled very weakly at him.

'You all right, San? You've gone ever so white,' said Kim, peering at me.

I nodded, not feeling strong enough for speech.

'Liven up then,' Kim whispered. 'Roy will think he's lumbered with a real dumbo unless you start chatting a bit.'

I stared at her in mute fury and concentrated on taking great gulps of fresh air. I didn't want to go into the pub. I knew I looked even younger than fifteen and I might easily get turfed straight out again. I felt terribly self-conscious as we went and sat down in the saloon. I didn't have a clue what drink to ask for. I'd only ever had coke or lemonade when I'd sat in pub gardens with Mum and Stan. I wondered what Kim would drink. Something sophisticated, like Campari and soda?

It was a relief when she asked for a half of shandy. I asked for a cider. I felt in my bag for my purse with Stan's money but the boys paid for the drinks. Only they weren't boys. They seemed to be getting older all the time. They stood at the bar together, sipping their pints.

'What's *up* with you, San?' said Kim, crossing her legs petulantly. 'You don't look as if you're enjoying yourself.'

'I'm not.'

'What? Oh San. Come on. He's not that bad.'

'He is.'

'Well, he's better than nothing.'

'No, I'd much sooner nothing.'

'I don't know what's up with you, I really don't. I thought I was doing you this great big favour.'

'Thank *you*.'

'Anyway, there's no need to mess things up for me. You sitting there with a face like that puts the mockers on everything. Cheer up, for God's sake. Look, they're coming over with our drinks. Get a few ciders inside you and get a bit merry.'

I got several ciders inside me but I didn't feel at all merry. After a while Jeff stopped discussing football and cars with Roy and turned his attention to Kim. She snuggled up to him, laughing obligingly at almost everything he said. Roy and I sat separate and silent.

At last he said, aggressively, 'You don't say much, do you?'

'Neither do you.'

Our conversation did not sparkle. I knew how stupid we must look, sitting sullen and apart, while Kim and Jeff performed animatedly. Roy had stopped winking but he chewed at his lips. He tried to beat time with his foot to the taped music but he couldn't get the right rhythm.

'Where do you work, Roy?' I said desperately.

'The Fullwell works.'

'Oh, I know. What do you do then?'

'I'm a fitter, aren't I?'

'What does a fitter do?'

'How do you mean?'

'Well, what exactly do you do?'

'You're a right nosy bird, aren't you?'

I wanted to punch him on his pimply nose but I forced myself to giggle, as if he'd paid me a compliment.

'Have you got a car too?'

'No. I've got a motor bike.'

'Have you? Do you go very fast?'

'It's busted.'

'Did you have a crash?'

'No, the engine's just all to cock.'

One last try.

'Whereabouts do you live?'

'Mallington.'

'Do you live with your parents or have you got your own place or what?'

'I live with my Mum and my step-Dad.'

It was the first thing he'd said that interested me.

'How do you get on with him?'

'Who?'

'Your stepfather.'

He shrugged. 'Don't see much of him, do I?'

'I've got a stepfather too. I can't stand him.'

Roy thawed a little. 'Why's that then?'

'He's an absolute pig. He even looks like a pig, all big and pink and porky, with a huge backside.'

'Yeah?' he said encouragingly.

'He's got a terrible temper too.'

'Knock you about a bit, does he?'

I hesitated. 'Yes, not half.'

'That's rotten that. Hitting a kid like you. What does your old lady say?'

'My Mum? She doesn't care. She's always on his side. The minute I'm old enough, I'm leaving.'

'That's right, get a bit of freedom. I'm thinking of leaving home myself. Emigrating.'

'Really. Where? Australia?'

'No. Canada. Where my old man is.'

'Your father?'

'I'm thinking of joining up with him. Sounds a great life out there. Better than this dump.'

'When did he go out to Canada then?'

'I dunno. When I was a little kid.'

'He split up with your Mum then?'

'Yeah. I expect he couldn't stand her nagging. No effing wonder.'

'But he left you behind?'

'Me and my sisters. Well, he couldn't take us, could he? What would he want to saddle himself with three whiny kids for?'

'Didn't you mind, him walking out on you?'

'I was too little to remember much. It used to bother me sometimes, I suppose. My Mum used to carry on about him, making out he was worse than Jack the bleeding Ripper. But then I started thinking things out for myself. I was only hearing her side of it, wasn't I?'

'Yes, I suppose so,' I said thoughtfully. I took a long gulp of cider. 'Yes. You've got a point, Roy.'

Kim nudged me. 'Come on then, San. We're starving. Let's go and eat, eh?'

I looked at my watch. It was twenty past nine.

'Will there be time?'

'Don't be a twit! Of course there's time. Come on.'

It felt cold out after the heat of the pub. Jeff took off his suit jacket and wrapped it round Kim's shoulders.

'Here, you want my jacket round you?' said Roy.

I didn't want his jacket at all and insisted I was very warm but Roy draped it over me all the same. Kim looked cute but I knew I just looked silly. The jacket smelt of aftershave and sweat. I felt as if Roy himself was wrapped right round me and my skin prickled. I hated the idea of his smell permeating the material of my shirt. He held my hand in the car. Both our hands were unpleasantly moist. My wrist was at an uncomfortable angle but I didn't like to fidget.

'Here, who bites their nails then?' he said.

My hand was trapped so I couldn't hide my stubby fingers.

'How old are you, Sandy?' said Roy.

'She's sixteen, same as me,' Kim said quickly.

'Sweet sixteen. The age of consent, eh?' said Jeff, turning round and grinning at Roy. Roy winked back.

My heart started thudding. I wasn't sure if they were just making silly jokes or if they were serious. I wondered if Kim had ever done it with Jeff. Her friend Debra was supposed to have slept with half the neighbourhood. Ages ago, when we were best friends, Kim always said she didn't fancy the idea of sex at all and she wasn't going to sleep with anyone until she was at least engaged. But that was when she still had her hair in bunches and wore kneesocks to school. She'd changed so much. I'd shocked her in those days, because I said I thought sex sounded lovely and that I was looking forward to having lovers. I still quite liked the idea of sex but I didn't feel ready for a lover. Certainly not a lover like Roy.

We went to a crowded American hamburger place. There were a lot of students from the Poly sitting near us so I was surrounded by flesh and blood versions of my intellectual fantasy Roy. I imagined them looking in our direction and sneering. We seemed so much sillier and spottier. Jeff and Kim kept messing about with the relish tray, twirling it round and flicking little flecks of sauce and pickle at each other. Kim had had quite a few shandies by this time and screamed with laughter. I grew hot with embarrassment. Roy stared at Kim and I thought he might be embarrassed too, but he said, 'She's got a smashing personality, your friend, hasn't she?'

I left half my hamburger and didn't want anything else, but Jeff insisted we all had a huge Knickerbocker Glory. I thought of the long drive back home and wondered how I was ever going to make it without being sick. I looked at my watch. An entire hour had whizzed past.

'Kim! It's twenty past ten,' I hissed. 'We'd better get going.'

'What? What are you on about? We haven't even had our coffee yet. Stop fussing, San.'

'But I told my Mum, remember? I've got to be back by half past ten.'

She stared at me as if I was mad.

'Yes, but she doesn't really expect you back then, does she?'

'Yes!'

'What are you two girls whispering about?' said Jeff.

'It's San,' said Kim, pouting. 'She wants to go home.'

'It's just that I'm supposed to be back by half past ten,' I said, blushing.

'Jesus,' said Roy, raising his eyebrows.

'We'll get you home, sweetheart, don't you worry,' said Jeff. 'Trust your Uncle Jeff, eh?'

I didn't trust my Uncle Jeff at all, but there didn't seem to be any alternative. Well, I *could* have walked out of the restaurant and caught a bus home, I suppose. Only it would have been so embarrassing and I'd made such a fool of myself already. So I sat it out, my stomach churning, while the others had coffee. Roy put two cigarettes in his mouth at once, lit them both, and passed one to me. I didn't see how I could refuse it when it was already lit. It would have sabotaged the whole flamboyant gesture. So I took occasional nervous puffs, screwing up my eyes against the smoke, while the minute hand raced round my watch at an alarming rate.

It was nearly eleven o'clock when we left the restaurant and I knew there was going to be a terrible row. Mum always worries if I'm even five minutes late home from school. Stan wouldn't worry about me, of course, but he'd be furious because Mum was upset. I'd never be able to make them see that it wasn't my fault.

I was so busy praying that I wasn't going to be car sick that I was taken by surprise when Jeff drew up down by the river.

'Where are we?' I said, bewildered.

'Oh San!' said Kim, giggling, as she leant back against the door invitingly.

'She's a bit slow, your mate, isn't she?' Jeff whispered, practically lying on top of Kim. 'This is bleeding uncomfortable. Bloody gears. It's all right for them in the back seat, eh?'

Roy and I were not making the most of our superior

24

seating arrangements. We sat at least a foot apart, silent and still, while Kim and Jeff wriggled and sighed and panted in front of us. My cheeks were burning. I didn't think they were actually making love, but they seemed alarmingly carried away. I wondered how they could bear to do it with us as silent witnesses.

'It's very quiet in the back,' Jeff said. 'What are they up to then, eh?'

Kim giggled and then they started another passionate embrace. Roy was suddenly spurred into action. He leant across the seat, held me by the scruff of my neck, and started kissing me. Kim giggled again and Jeff mumbled something I couldn't catch. Roy's mouth was very moist and his teeth were very hard. I tried to keep my own mouth clamped together but his tongue came slithering through my lips. I hated it but I didn't like to push Roy away in case he thought I was objecting to his spots. I was glad it was too dark to see them clearly.

After a while Roy's other hand plucked ineffectually at my waist and then started creeping upwards. When it was within an inch of my right breast I grabbed it and pushed it back down to my waist. If I'd had a respectable size breast I might have let Roy touch it, but I was far too ashamed of my inadequacy to let him discover it. After I'd fielded his hand several times it decided on a new tactic and fastened itself in a clammy fashion to my knee. My leg was bare above my socks. The hand crawled upwards and I panicked. What was I doing, letting a strange man I didn't even like mess about with my body?

'Don't!'

Roy sighed ostentatiously and pulled away from me. He lit a cigarette, not bothering to offer me one this time. We waited until Kim and Jeff drew apart and lit cigarettes too.

I took a deep breath.

'I've really *got* to get home.'

The lights were still on when Jeff drove up outside my house. I could see Mum at the window, peering anxiously round the curtain, and then the door opened and Stan stood there. I stumbled out of the car. Roy didn't even bother to say goodbye to me. The car drove off before I'd even reached the garden gate. Stan ran down the path towards me.

'Where the hell have you been? It's gone midnight! How dare you worry us sick like this?'

But I was also worried sick. I clamped my hand over my mouth, dodged past Stan, ran to the bathroom and vomited.

# *Chapter 4*

'"*H*ELLO," Rosamund whispered shyly. Her father smiled back at her. The sun shone on his thick greying curls, his lean tanned face. He held out his arms. Rosamund clung to him, her face buried in his Guernsey sweater. "You don't know just how much I've longed for this moment," he said in his attractively husky voice. "Welcome home."'

I sighed with satisfaction and laid down my pen. I read through the whole story excitedly. It was good, I was sure of it. And the ending was perfect. Even better than the affair with the addict poet in the middle. It was very long too, more than twenty pages. Perhaps they'd be so impressed that they'd ask me to expand it a little and turn it into a proper novel.

I leant back in my chair and day-dreamed about the reviews. 'This novel would be an impressive achievement by any standards, but when one remembers that it was written by a fifteen-year-old schoolgirl then one is taken aback by the maturity and sophistication of the style and plot. . . .' Yes. And then perhaps television? An interview with Robert Robinson or Melvyn Bragg? I'd wear my hair tied up artistically and I'd have to have a new dress, maybe one of those beautiful embroidered dresses in that lovely Monsoon shop. I'd be able to afford it because the novel would make me heaps of money. Enough to buy my own place, my romantic Victorian attic flat, and because I'd proved I was so grown-up for my age I could live there on my own and not have to bother with school and O-levels. And then . . . then *my* father, my real father, would go into a bookshop one day and pick up a copy of my novel and read it and be absolutely

27

transfixed and then stare at the photograph on the back and realise . . . and he'd come and find me and we'd live together in my attic, or perhaps he'd have somewhere of his own, a lovely old house in the country, yes, so we could spend the week-ends there. . . .

'Finished the masterpiece?' said Mum, coming up behind me and making me jump. 'Hey, you've written an awful lot.'

She was trying to make friends with me. There had been an awful row last night. They even blamed me for being sick, thinking I'd had too much to drink. And then Stan started it all over again this morning, just because I had a bit of a lie-in and Mum brought me up a cup of tea.

'Lying there like Lady Muck, expecting your poor mother to run round after you when she's been up half the night making herself ill with worry. . . .' He went on for hours. I just stared at his pointed piggy ears and his big snout nose and the coarse bristles on his chin and let him grunt and gobble without deigning to reply.

We had pork for lunch and he gnawed on his piece of crackling with cannibalistic greed. He put me off my own meal and then yelled at me because I wouldn't eat. Mum started sticking up for me a bit then, and said he couldn't expect me to eat much, not with an upset stomach, and he said that it was my own bloody fault I had an upset stomach and went over last night's row word for word.

I ended up in tears in my room but when I heard Stan go off with Julie to feed the ducks I went downstairs and helped Mum with the washing-up. Stan and Julie's little jaunts often lasted a couple of hours so I got on with my competition story while Mum made a trifle for tea.

The smell of strawberry jelly seeped through the house, obliterating the stink of pork. Mum and I had once eaten a whole strawberry jelly raw. She had given me a cube to chew and had one herself while she boiled the water, and then we'd had another cube each and then another, and then she took the water off the boil and poured it away and we gobbled up the rest of the jelly.

'Remember the time we ate that jelly straight from the packet?' I said.

Mum smiled. 'Fancy you remembering that. You were only about four or five.'

'Of course I can remember it. I can remember heaps of things.'

Mum sat down at the table with me and sighed.

'Thank God those days are over,' she said. 'It was tough on you, Sandra, I know.'

'I didn't mind. I liked it then. Before you got married.'

'Oh dear. I don't know what to do about you and Stan. I used to think in time . . . and yet it's got worse as you've got older. You're both fine when you're apart but when you're together – streuth! You seem to set each other off. I always end up the piggy in the middle, and it's no joke, I can tell you.'

'I can't see why he can't just leave me alone.'

'Oh Sandra!'

'Well, he's not my father, is he? He hasn't got the right to keep ordering me about.'

'Of course he's got the right. Now don't start again, please.'

'Do you ever think about my real father?' I couldn't believe I'd actually said it. I looked down at my story, fiddling with the corners of the pages. I heard Mum take a deep breath.

'No,' she said at last. 'No, of course I don't.'

'Did you ever though? Before you met Stan, say?'

'Well. Sometimes, I suppose.'

'Did you wish he'd married you?'

'Oh Sandra, don't let's go into all that now. Come on, I'll find you a big envelope for that story and we'll get it sent off.'

'Mum. Please. I want to talk about him. I've got a right to know a bit about him, haven't I?'

'I've never kept anything from you,' Mum said stiffly, but she put her elbows on the table, propping her chin in her hands. 'Well, what do you want to know?'

I wriggled. There were a hundred things and yet I couldn't think what was most important. I knew a few simple facts. My father's name is David Pilbeam. He met my mother when they were both very young, Mum got pregnant. David Pilbeam didn't want to know. Mum's parents were horrified and packed her off to a Mother and Baby Home. Mum was supposed to have me adopted but when I was born she couldn't go through with it.

'Did he ever see me?'

'No.'

'Didn't he want to?'

'How should I know? Anyway, that Home I was in, it was a good fifty miles away. And then afterwards I went to London.'

'Did you send him your address?'

'No, of course not. I was moving about a lot at that time. There was that awful living-in job at Hampstead, and then I went to Surbiton but that only lasted a couple of months, and then . . . did I go to those digs in Wimbledon then, or did we have the bedsit in Earl's Court?'

'So he didn't really know where you were.'

'Well?'

'He might have wanted to get in touch, mightn't he? And even your parents didn't know where you were at that time, did they?'

I didn't like calling them my grandparents. Mum had made it up with them when she met Stan. They came to the wedding and I stayed with them while Mum and Stan went away for their honeymoon. It was only a long week-end but it felt like a lifetime. My grandfather said nothing at all to me. My grandmother said far too much, nagging about my table manners and my bitten fingernails and my cheeky tone of voice. They lived near the sea so Mum had packed my bucket and spade, not bothering with any of my toys, but my grandma said there was oil on the beach and she wasn't going to have me trekking it in onto her good carpets.

She took me to the shops and bought me a baby doll with her own white attaché case containing a change of clothes and a nappy and a tiny brush and comb set. I dressed and undressed her many times and then her arm suddenly came off as I pushed it into her sleeve. My grandma went all white and pinched and said there was absolutely no point in buying me nice things if I couldn't look after them properly.

She managed to manipulate the arm back into its socket and the doll seemed as good as new but I didn't dare undress her any more. Then the next morning I broke the little plastic comb as I dragged it through the baby doll's curls and I spent the rest of my visit hot with dread in case my grandma found out. The doll was very pretty but her little painted mouth was in the shape of a sneer and when Mum came for me at last, I squashed the doll inside her own attaché case and never played with her again.

I only saw Mum's parents twice after that, and one of those times was my grandma's funeral. She died of cancer and then six months later my grandpa started to get similar symptoms and got so frightened that he took an overdose of sleeping pills and killed himself.

I couldn't understand why my mother was so upset. She cried on and off for weeks, particularly after my grandfather died. She said she should have gone to see him more often, maybe even offered him a home with us. I thought that was extraordinary, when he had practically told her never to darken his doors again. I still found it hard to believe that they had been so incredibly callous to my mother and had sent her off all by herself when she was only eighteen months older than me. I didn't give a damn that they'd died. But even now I saw Mum's eyes were suspiciously watery.

'My father might have changed his mind,' I persisted. 'Perhaps he might have wanted to marry you, once I was actually born.'

'Well, he couldn't. He was going on to university. He was much cleverer than me, Sandra. He was a different sort of lad. I was right out of my depth with him.'

'Did you really love him?'

Mum shrugged. 'You don't know what love is, not at that age,' she said.

'But you thought you loved him?'

'Of course I did. Otherwise I wouldn't have . . . well, you know.'

'You hadn't ever done it with anyone else then?'

'Sandra! Look, you're going too far. Don't take advantage.

I'm trying to talk to you seriously. Of course I hadn't done it with anyone else. What do you take me for, eh?'

'Sorry. I didn't mean. . . .'

'Yes. Well. If you must know I fell for you the very first time.'

'Really!'

'Really.'

'But didn't you know about contraception in those days?'

'In those days! You make it sound like the Middle Ages. Yes, we did know, but it wasn't so easy then. Well, not for my sort of girl. I mean, my parents never told me a thing and we just learnt about animals at school. Rabbits don't go on the Pill or use French Letters, do they? What are you grinning at, eh? It might seem funny now but by God it didn't seem much of a joke at the time.'

'What did you do when you knew for sure you were going to have me?'

'I didn't do anything, not for ages. I just kept quiet and willed it not to be true.'

'But then you told my father?'

'Eventually.'

'Where?'

'Mm?'

'Where did you tell him? Did you go round to his house or what?'

'No! I never set foot in his house. I doubt if I'd have been welcome. His parents really fancied themselves. I think his dad was a solicitor and his mother was on all sorts of committees, you know the type. I was just a silly little girl from the council estate, wasn't I? No, I met him at a coffee bar place and told him there.'

'And what did he say?'

'What? Oh, I can't remember, not after all this time.'

'I bet you can.'

'He didn't really know what to say. And then – oh God, I hate thinking about it.'

'What? Was he horrible to you?'

'No. No, he – he burst into tears. Right there in the coffee bar, with everyone looking. I didn't know where to put myself.'

'Did he!' Mum sounded ashamed but I was very touched. He'd actually cried. That meant he must have cared. He was sensitive and emotional.

'I don't know why he did the crying. I was the one who was well and truly lumbered, not him,' Mum said bitterly.

'It showed he was sorry, surely.'

'It was a bit late for being sorry. I could have done with a bit of constructive help. I wanted him to be a bit manly, not act all wet and cry. I didn't cry once, not the whole time.'

'I cry a lot. Do you think I take after him?'

'Yes, you do a bit.'

'Really?'

'Not so much in looks. But in character, in some ways. And you're bright at school, aren't you, like him. It's funny you're so keen on writing because he was too.'

I stared at her. 'Why ever didn't you tell me before?'

'You never asked, did you? He was going to do English at university.'

'Which university?'

'I don't know. He wanted to be a writer though. He was writing a book himself. He read me a bit of it. I thought it was ever so outspoken, but I wasn't really any sort of judge.'

'And did he ever get it published?'

'Well, how would I know? I wouldn't be a bit surprised. He wrote me this great long letter after I'd told him I was in trouble. Twelve or fourteen pages long, it took me hours reading it. There were even bits of poetry.'

'Can I see it?'

'I haven't still got it.'

'You don't mean you actually threw it away!'

'Of course I did. Well, I did hang on to it for a while, if you must know. Quite a long while. But when I met Stan and made a whole new start I chucked a lot of stuff out. I had a photo of him but I'm afraid I threw that out too.'

'Oh no.'

'I'm sorry. I suppose I should have kept it for you but I

didn't think. Maybe I was hoping that you'd look on Stan as your real father.'

'What?'

'He's tried his hardest to be a proper dad to you, Sandra, so you can wipe that look off your face for a start. Couldn't you try a bit harder with him? To please me? Can't you see the difference Stan's made to us? Both of us. You say you can remember all what happened to you when you were little. Well, it was no picnic, right? And you don't know the half of what I went through then. I still have nightmares about it. You've no idea how wonderful it is to wake up and feel Stan beside me and realise I don't have to worry any more.'

'Is that why you married him then, Mum? So you wouldn't have to worry?'

'I married Stan because I loved him,' Mum said quietly.

There was a pause. Mum picked up my competition story.

'I'll find a big envelope,' she said. 'I've got the address tucked away somewhere too, I'll do it all for you. Now, is there anything good on the telly? Stan and Julie should be back soon.'

I went upstairs to lie on my bed and mull over what she'd told me. I kept imagining that scene in the coffee bar when my mother told my father she was going to have me. It was weird trying to picture Mum looking only a little older than me, and my father as a boy of eighteen. How could my mother have been stupid enough to be embarrassed by his tears? I couldn't get over the incredible fact that he'd wanted to be a writer too. If only they'd both been a bit older. Say when my father had just got his university degree. Then he'd have been able to marry my mother and I'd have been Sandra Pilbeam. Maybe not even Sandra. My father might have chosen my name. He'd have read to me when I was little. Maybe even made up special stories for me. And then as I grew older he'd have encouraged me to do well at school. He'd have wanted to read all my stories and poems and been proud of me. If only, if only, if only. . . .

I got a piece of paper and some Sellotape and started making myself a fortune dice. I wrote 'YES', 'ALMOST CERTAIN', 'PROBABLY', 'POSSIBLY', 'VERY DOUBTFUL' and 'NO' on the six sides of my paper dice. I've often made myself a fortune dice and asked it all sorts of questions. Things like: 'Will I ever get a proper boyfriend?' and 'Will my breasts ever get any bigger?' and 'Will it rain tomorrow so I don't have to play hockey?' I know it's only a silly game of chance but it's easy to take it seriously.

I asked it just two questions. 'Will I win the story competition?' 'Will I ever get to meet my real father?'

Would you believe that against all the odds that dice said 'YES' both times?

# *Chapter 5*

---

$S$IX weeks later a white envelope skimmed through the letter-box and landed on the hall carpet. I saw the name of the firm running the story competition in the right-hand corner of the envelope and I started shaking. I held it against my chest for a moment, my eyes squeezed shut, and then I tore it open. My eyes slid wildly down the black mass of typescript and saw WINNER OF YOUR AGE GROUP. My arms prickled with goose-flesh. I shivered, shaking my head, and then I gave a whoop and started leaping about the hall in my dressing-gown. My slippers flew off as I kicked up my legs. I pulled out my dressing-gown cord and whirled it over my head like a lasso.

'Sandra! What on earth are you up to?' Mum came out of the kitchen and stared at me. Julie came rushing too and shrieked with laughter.

'Hey, Daddy, come and look at Sandra,' she said, trying to catch me.

For once I didn't push her away. I put my arms round her chest and twirled round with me while she squeaked with excitement. Stan came and watched, his arm round my mother.

'What's going on then?' he said, smiling expectantly.

I smiled back at him, so happy that I wanted Stan to be part of it too.

'I've won the writing competition. I'm the winner in my age group,' I said. 'I've won it, I've won it, I've actually won it!'

'Oh Sandra! Isn't that marvellous,' said Mum. 'Mind

you, you did work hard on that story, and it was ever so long. Oh, I'm so proud of you.'

'What do you get for winning then? What sort of prizes are there?' said Stan.

'I don't know! Wait a minute, perhaps it'll say,' I said, looking at the letter again.

Then I read it properly. Carefully. Every word of it.

'Well, what have you won, lovie?' said Mum.

'Nothing.'

'What?'

'That's a fat lot of use,' said Stan. 'That's not much of a competition if you ask me.'

'Nobody is asking you, you fat pig,' I shouted.

'Sandra! What is it? What's wrong?' said Mum.

'It's all right, you can all go on celebrating,' I said, tears trickling down my cheeks. 'I haven't won the competition, but *she* has. It's her letter, not mine.'

I flung it at Julie and rushed upstairs to my bedroom. I got right back into bed, not even bothering to take my dressing-gown off first, and huddled into a tight ball, my chin on my knees. I had the covers pulled right up over my head. It was dark and stifling and silent. I didn't make a sound but tears leaked from my eyes and dribbled across my face onto the pillow.

I knew I was behaving very badly. If I'd had any pride or dignity at all then I'd have pretended not to care, maybe even managed to congratulate Julie. But knowing I was acting like a spoilt baby didn't help me get up and face them. I wanted to stay wilting in the moist tropical heat of my bed for ever.

Mum left me for a good half-hour and then she knocked on my bedroom door. I heard her, smothered as I was, but I didn't say anything.

'Sandra? Hey, Sandra lovie, don't take it to heart so.' I heard her cross the room to my bed, and then a hand gently patted the covers. I grimaced under the blanket, sweating with embarrassment and shame. I held onto the edge of the bedclothes in case she was going to pull them off me, but she left them alone and sat at the end of my bed.

'It's all right, love. We understand.'

I knew they understood. Somehow that made it worse. I felt painfully exposed, my skin ripped right off to show my puny muscles and brittle bones. They knew how badly I wanted to be a writer. They knew this competition had meant a great deal to me. They knew I could have been reasonably philosophical if anyone else had won. But not Julie. And it wasn't even as if she was precociously gifted at writing. When I was her age I'd made up all sorts of imaginary friends and could play happily for ages all by myself. I'd already learnt to read fluently but I often preferred looking at illustrations in old magazines and making up my own stories.

But Julie's still at the pointing finger monotone stage of reading and she never writes more than a couple of sentences in her workbook at school. I'd seen what she'd written on the back of her hand picture. I didn't think it was particularly inspiring.

'My Dad has big hands to do the work.
My Mum has soft hands to do the cudling.
Sandra has inky hands to do the riting.
I have litel hands to do the playing.'

What's so special about that? I'm sure any kid who's nearly six could do that sort of thing. They called it a poem in that awful letter. Well, Julie certainly didn't set out to write a poem. They also said it was delightfully original. That's nonsense too, because I'm sure she got the soft hands bit from that sickly television commercial about washing-up liquid. Mum hasn't got soft hands anyway, they're quite rough because she can't be bothered with rubber gloves or hand cream.

'I wish you could have won, Sandra. I know it meant so much to you. And you wrote such a lot too, page after page. It seems so unfair when Julie didn't try hard at all.'

I grunted, knowing I would have to surface soon.

'I only put her little piece in the envelope as an afterthought. I don't really know what made me do it. I never thought in a million years that our Julie would get anywhere.'

I squeezed myself hard and then managed to mumble, 'Well, she did. So I suppose I'd better go and congratulate the infant prodigy.'

I managed to do it with relative grace. I even apologised to Stan for calling him a fat pig. But it didn't get any easier. A newspaper reporter came to do an interview with Julie. She insisted on wearing her party frock and a pair of Mum's high heeled shoes and showed off disgustingly but the reporter lapped up her performance. Then she was asked to go on local radio to read out her so-called masterpiece. She sounded even younger on the radio and giggled and lisped in nauseating baby fashion, but everyone seemed to think she was really fetching.

It was the summer holidays, but some girls in my class at school came over to my house just to see 'Little Julie' and give her their congratulations. They stood round her admiringly, watching her as if she was a tiny television set. They all said she was *sweet* and they'd give anything to have a little sister like her.

Mum still tried to be tactful, at least when I was around, but Stan soon stopped soft-pedalling his praises and made much of Julie, calling her his little Agatha Christie. She is probably the only female writer Stan has ever heard of. Julie got a pen and pencil set and a five pound book token for winning the 5–8 year old section of the competition, but Stan didn't think this generous enough.

'We ought to celebrate. After all, it was a nationwide competition, and thousands of kiddies entered. Fancy our Julie knocking them all into a cocked hat. And now she's turning into a right little celebrity, aren't you, poppet? Want to hear yourself on the radio again, eh?' Stan had taped Julie's two minute interview and had played it so often we could chant it by heart. He listened again nevertheless and switched off the tape with a contented sigh.

'Yes, like I said, this calls for a celebration. So I've booked for us all to go for a meal on Saturday.'

'Oh Dad, are we going to a McDonalds? Goody-goody!' Julie trilled.

'No, my lovely, none of your hamburgers on Saturday. We're doing things in style. I've booked up at the Milano.'

'Oh Stan! You want your brains testing. Not *the* Milano, the Italian place near the river?' said Mum.

'The one and only.'

'But it costs a fortune. I was talking to a woman who went there on her wedding anniversary and it was nearly thirty pounds just for the two of them.'

'Look, I don't care how much it costs. How often does our Julie win a competition like this, eh? Don't spoil things, Mary, please. I've booked, and it's all settled. We're going to have the time of our lives on Saturday,' Stan ordered.

I didn't want to go but I didn't dare be difficult this time. I even got myself all tarted up in my long Laura Ashley dress for the occasion. Julie wore her party frock again, with a pink angora bolero. Stan called her his little bunny so Julie went round twitching her nose in a twee imitation of a rabbit. Mum wore her grey silky blouse and a long, black, velvet skirt. She'd have looked quite nice but she's put on too much weight for the skirt so her tummy bulged unbecomingly and her blouse buttons kept coming undone.

'Once I've had my lovely meal tonight I really must go on a diet,' she said, but Stan told her she was talking nonsense and when he thought I wasn't looking he put his hands on her breasts and whispered something to her. I felt sick, wondering how she could bear him pawing her in such a crude way.

I remembered Roy's hands in the back of the car. I hadn't heard any more from him, of course. Kim had gone out of her way to avoid me at school. She'd obviously told Debra all about it because whenever I went past they nudged each other and giggled, and once they muttered something about football socks and then burst out laughing.

It didn't look as if I was ever going to get myself a proper boy-friend. I was sure I was the only fifteen-year-old in the whole town going out with Mummy, Stepdaddy and little sister on Saturday night. Stan parked the car in the big multi-storey so we had to walk right through the town centre to the Milano. I saw several girls from my school. They were all with boys, apart from a giggly group of second years, and at least they didn't have their parents with them. I tried hanging back, walking three or four paces behind Mum and Stan and Julie so that people might not realise I was with them, but Mum kept on turning round and telling me to catch up. Mum and I looked foolish in our long skirts, like bridesmaids who'd lost their wedding.

It was a relief when we actually got inside the Milano – but not for long. We were all overawed by the general gloom of the restaurant and the gleam of the glasses and cutlery. Mum got flustered when a waiter helped her into her chair and stood on her skirt. Julie kept playing with her place-mat and napkin and knife and fork, but when I told her to leave them alone Stan told me she wasn't doing any harm. So Julie went on fiddling, and as soon as she'd been given her glass of coke she knocked it flying. Mum nearly died and tried to mop the table-cloth. Stan kept hissing at her to leave it. Julie looked anxious, as if she might be on the brink of tears. I sipped my grapefruit juice in silence, although I could have said a lot.

'Right. What grub are we all having?' said Stan, over-heartily. 'What about you, Julie? What does my little pal want, eh?'

'Hamburger and chips, please,' said Julie.

'No pet, you don't get that sort of food here,' Mum said quickly. 'You get much nicer special food. Now, let Mummy see what you'd like. Thank heavens they've got the English printed under all that twirly Italian writing, we'd have been right up the creek otherwise. Ah, how about having chicken in a nice sauce?'

'I want a hamburger and chippies.'

'They don't *do* hamburgers, I just told you.'

'Then I'll just have chips. Lots of chips.'

'Julie,' Mum said warningly, but Stan interrupted, trying not to look put out.

'Let the kiddie have what she fancies, Mary. We'll get lots of chips, Julie, don't you worry. And how about some fish to go with them, eh? And a prawn cocktail for starters. You know them little baby pink fishies, you like them.'

It turned out she didn't like them at all, because she didn't like the sauce they were in, and she didn't think much of her fish either, because it wasn't in familiar orange bread-crumbs. So she just ate her chips, one by one, with her fingers. Mum was so fraught that I don't think she even tasted her own chicken. Stan made a great to-do over his peppered steak, saying it was superb and kissing his fingers theatrically, but it was still bloody inside and I could see he had to make a conscious effort to get it down.

I thought my own meal was wonderful. Well, perhaps I'm not so sure about my avocado pear. Is it really supposed to taste of nothing at all? Perhaps that's why they put that vinegary stuff all over it. But I truly enjoyed my own chicken in its wine sauce. Mum let me have a glass of white wine to go with it. I concentrated hard on my meal, trying to blot out Mum and Stan and Julie, pretending I was there with somebody intelligent and gentle and sensitive. A lover? No, Roy had made me feel queasy about sex. Then how about my father? He'd managed to trace me at long last and this was our first meal together, and now we'd finished our main course he took my hand and squeezed it and told me he was so happy he'd found me and he never wanted to let me out of his sight and I was just the sort of daughter he'd always longed for. . . .

'Come on, Sandra. Do stop sulking,' Mum hissed. 'Couldn't you make a bit of an effort for once? We all know you're upset because you didn't win the wretched competition but it's about time you grew up a bit and stopped being such a baby.'

I was so taken aback I couldn't even think what to say. I *hadn't* been sulking. How dare she pick on me, when it was Julie who was behaving atrociously, rocking on her chair and blowing bubbles in her drink and taking a bite out of every bread stick on the table. I could see Mum was itching to give her a good smack, but if Julie started howling then Stan could no longer pretend that his expensive celebratory evening was a success. But why take it out on me? All right, if they thought I was sulking then I jolly well would sulk, and to hell with them all.

I decided not to do myself out of a pudding, however, and enjoyed my strawberries and cream. Julie started whining for strawberries too. She'd chosen a huge, creamy chocolate cake but only ate a mouthful, insisting it was bad. Stan wanted to make a fuss, saying he was damned if he was going to spend a small fortune on a bit of cake if the cream was off, but Mum tasted it and said the cream was fine, it was the liqueur flavouring that Julie didn't like.

Julie wriggled about on her seat, yawning and rubbing her eyes because it was now long past her bedtime. Mum eventually took her on her lap and let her have several spoonfuls of sugar just to keep her quiet. I kept quiet too, determined not to say a word.

But I couldn't help saying something when it came to paying the bill. Stan laid a handful of fivers on the plate with studied nonchalance, and then put two ten pence pieces beside his coffee cup. I stared at them unbelievingly. Mum didn't even notice, too busy wiping round Julie's sticky mouth and getting her to put her cardigan on.

'Stan. You put more than that,' I whispered urgently.

'What?'

'The tip! The service isn't included, it says so on the menu. You have to give about fifteen percent of the bill.'

'You don't *have* to give a brass farthing,' said Stan. 'You just mind your own business, eh?'

'But you *can't* just leave twenty pence! What on earth will they think? Mum, he can't, can he?'

She hesitated uneasily.

'I don't give a bugger what they think – or you either,' said Stan. 'Come on, let's get out of this place. It's not all it's cracked up to be. If you ask me they're bloody lucky to get twenty pee.'

The waiter took the plate away and looked pointedly at the two coins on the table-cloth. I burned with humiliation and hatred for Stan. We shuffled out of the restaurant, Julie telling everyone at the top of her voice that she needed a wee-wee.

She managed to hold out for the car journey but wet herself going up the garden path. I stalked past in disgust and let myself in with my own key. I was half-way up the stairs when Mum called me.

'Here, Sandra, put these into soak for me, eh?' She held out Julie's sopping knickers.

'No!'

'Well, will you run a bath for her then? Come on, she's tired out and I want to get her to bed quick.'

'Look, I'm not the general servant. Why should I run round after Julie?'

Mum sucked in her breath. 'All right, don't. My God, you're turning into a selfish little madam. You get taken out for a beautiful meal like that and yet you won't do the slightest little thing to help.'

'But it wasn't beautiful at all. Why's everyone keeping up the pretence? The entire evening was a disaster. Julie certainly didn't enjoy herself. She'd have been much happier at a McDonalds – and you don't leave tips there, so Stan wouldn't have embarrassed us all.'

Mum came flying up the stairs and slapped me hard across the face.

I burst into tears. 'I hate you,' I shouted. 'And I hate that fat pig you married, and I hate your snivelling little brat too. I hate all of you.'

I ran to my room, slammed the door, yanked my suitcase down from the top of the wardrobe, and started throwing clothes into it.

# *Chapter 6*

*I* WANTED to run away but when my suitcase was full I
stood uncertainly in the middle of my room, not knowing
what to do. I had just over three pounds in my money-box. It
probably wasn't even enough for a room for the night. And
which room anyway? I didn't know any cheap hotels nearby.
I thought about getting a train to London but what was I
going to do once I was there? I knew there were supposed to
be evil men hanging around Waterloo and King's Cross,
ready to pick up teenage runaways and introduce them to a
life of vice, but I didn't think even they would fancy a skinny
girl with glasses and a flat chest. So I'd walk the streets all
night ignored by everyone, and I'd probably go on walking
the streets, day and night, eating out of litter-bins once my
three pounds nine and a half pence was spent, turning into
one of those mad, smelly, vagrant ladies in sacking and old
flapping boots. It was a daunting thought. So eventually I
unpacked my suitcase and undressed and got into bed. I
heard Mum putting Julie to bed and then a long while
afterwards she went up to bed herself with Stan, but she
didn't come into my room at all. She didn't even call out
good-night.

By the next morning I'd decided that I'd have to wait a
while before I could run away, but meanwhile I would not
have anything at all to do with my family. Normally in the
holidays I sleep late and then potter about the house and
maybe do a bit of school work or write my own stories or
whatever, and then I go out with Mum and Julie to the park
or the river in the afternoon. But I certainly wasn't going to
hang around them any more.

I got up early and went to the big library in the town centre, not my usual little branch library just down the road. I looked for a David Pilbeam book on the shelves but there weren't any, so I searched the card index system, both fiction and non-fiction, but there was no mention of a David Pilbeam there either. A pretty library assistant with glasses almost the same as mine asked if I needed any help.

'Have you ever heard of a writer called David Pilbeam?'

She thought and then shook her head. 'It doesn't ring a bell. What sort of things does he write?'

'I'm not sure. I don't know for certain that he's ever had anything published.'

'Well, let's look him up in the Books in Print catalogue.' She thumbed through a huge red book but couldn't find him there either.

'So he can't have ever written anything,' I said sadly.

'No, this just means that there's nothing of his in print. He could have written heaps of things for all we know. How did you hear about him? Did you see him on television or what?'

'No, he's just – just someone I once knew, a long time ago. He wanted to be a writer, you see. He'd started writing a book. But I don't know if he ever finished it. And I don't suppose there's any way of finding out.'

'Not unless you go to the British Museum.'

'Why there?'

'They've got a copy of every single book that's ever been published. They've got this huge reading room, it's famous.'

'I'll have to go there one day,' I said.

I went the very next day, deciding there was no point in wasting time. Mum and I were just about on speaking terms again and she looked surprised when I got my jacket and bag straight after breakfast.

'Are you off out again?'

'Yep.'

'Can't you wait ten minutes until I've got the washing-up done and then Julie and I will come with you. I've got to go into Marks for some new vests for Julie and then I wondered about trying that new coffee place –'

She was making conciliatory noises but I didn't want to be friends.

'I'm not going into the town, I'm going up to London.'

You'd have thought I'd announced I was going to the moon. She made a great fuss and in the end I lied and said I was going with Kim, because Mum would keep twittering on about not liking to think of me wandering around on my own, because you hear so many unpleasant things about London nowadays. Even when I'd got her convinced that I'd be with Kim she seemed very doubtful, worrying that we might get lost, run over or raped up a dark alleyway.

I was very scornful, but in actual fact I did have a horrible fumbly man sitting next to me on the tube, I very nearly got mown down by a taxi in Tottenham Court Road and I set off in entirely the wrong direction for the British Museum and got as far as Euston before realising my mistake. I was feeling pretty demoralized by the time I actually went up the steps of the British Museum and through the revolving doors. I'd never been there before. Mum and Stan had taken me round the Tower of London and Trafalgar Square and Madame Tussauds but never anywhere cultural.

I felt stupidly nervous, not quite sure how you were supposed to behave in museums, and I jumped when a man in uniform stopped me and asked to look in my bag. I thought I must have done something wrong, but he laughed.

'Don't look so worried, ducky. I just want to see you haven't got a bomb tucked in your bag, that's all.'

I let him peer inside and then I wandered around the entrance hall, trying to get my bearings. Luckily the Reading Room wasn't far away, but when I walked towards the door an attendant stopped me.

'I'm sorry, Miss. You can't go in there.'

I stared at him. 'But I want to look for a particular book,' I explained.

'You're not allowed in. You have to get special permission.'

'Can't you give me permission?'

'You have to be doing post-graduate research or something similar. You look a bit on the young side for that, Miss.'

'But I've come up to London specially. Couldn't I just have a very quick look, just to see if the book I want is there?'

'It's more than my job's worth to let you through that door. Now run away, there's a good girl.'

I trailed miserably away. All that train and tube money wasted! I decided that I might as well have a look round the museum while I was there so I wandered around the manuscript rooms. Any other time I would have been thrilled to see Lewis Carroll's own handwritten copy of *Alice* and Charlotte Brontë's neat copperplate and James Joyce's scribbled crossed out jottings for *Ulysses* (I'd furtively peeped in the Penguin paperback in Smiths because someone told me it had lots of very sexy bits, but I couldn't find any) but now I couldn't seem to care about them at all.

I went on to look at the illuminated manuscripts. We'd done the Middle Ages when I was in the first year and I'd been fascinated by the idea of monks working on a single manuscript for years. I'd even done some of my own rather wobbly illuminated letters with Windsor & Newton coloured inks and a mapping pen – but now I moved restlessly from one masterpiece to another, hardly giving them a glance. I walked more and more quickly, and then as I rounded a display cabinet I tripped over something down at my knees.

'Watch out, you great clumsy twit!'

It was a boy about a couple of years younger than me. He'd been crouching to do up the lace on his training shoes and I'd made him overbalance.

'I'm sorry,' I said, blushing. I felt as if I was burning all over. Then suddenly, before I could even turn away, my face screwed up and I burst into tears.

The boy gaped at me. I covered my face with my hands, horrified. I shut my eyes and bit hard on the inside of my cheeks, trying to stop these astonishing sobs.

'Have I hurt you or what?'

I shook my head, unable to explain. I moved away hurriedly, deciding to try to make for a Ladies, but the boy stuffed several notebooks in his plastic airline bag and trotted along beside me. People stared at us curiously. Tears still spilled down my cheeks and my nose started to run. I searched my pocket but couldn't find a tissue. I could feel mucus dribbling disgustingly from my nostril.

'Here, you'd better borrow my hanky.' The boy thrust it into my hand and I blew my nose.

'You're not upset just because I called you a clumsy twit, are you? Because I don't suppose it was really your fault. I shouldn't have bent over like that. Are you all right now?' He peered at me anxiously. He was a very old-fashioned looking boy, with short, badly cut hair, National Health glasses, and a hand-knitted red sweater that made him look very pale.

I wiped my eyes. 'Yes, I'm fine now. I'm sorry, I didn't mean to be such a baby. It was just . . . oh, I don't know. Thanks, anyway.' I held out his handkerchief but he didn't take it.

'You're supposed to offer to wash it for me, aren't you?' he said, grinning. 'That's what happens in all those corny old films. And I'm supposed to offer to buy you a coffee. Well, I wish I could, there's a good café here, only I haven't got enough money. Hint, hint.'

'What?' I stared at him blankly.

'Aren't you liberated enough to buy me a coffee? Although I'd sooner have a coke, if it's all the same.' He grinned at me hopefully.

I thought he had a bit of a cheek, but I had mucked up his handkerchief after all.

'All right then. Where's this café?'

'I'll show you. What's your name then?'

'Sandra.'

'It ought to be *Cas*sandra, the prophetess of doom. She liked a good wail too. My name's Michael. How old are you? Thirteen?'

'I'm fifteen,' I said indignantly.

'You don't look it. Oh well, never mind. I've always fancied older women.'

I stared at him. What was he, some kind of nut? He was only a silly little kid and yet he acted as if he was trying to chat me up.

He led me to the café and I bought us both a coke and a bag of crisps.

'Thanks. Only now I'm beginning to feel like a gigolo,' he said, tucking into his Smoky Bacons.

'A what?'

'Well, it's a male paid dancing partner, only now it's got sexual connotations,' he said airily.

I could feel myself going bright red again.

'Kid yourself!' I said. 'What does a little boy like you know about sex anyway?'

'I'm not a little boy at all. I'm fourteen. Well, nearly. And I'm very mature for my age.'

I spluttered into my coke. He was so little and puny he wouldn't have looked out of place in short trousers.

'I didn't necessarily mean physically mature,' he said with dignity. 'I happened to be referring to maturity of the intellect and emotions.'

'Oh yes?' I said weakly.

'Are you in the fourth year at school? Well, so am I. So that immediately establishes us on an equal footing.'

'You can't be in the fourth year, not if you're only thirteen.'

'I've been bumped up a couple of years. Honestly. You are talking to an intellectual phenomenon. I have an I.Q. of 156.'

'Is that supposed to impress me?' I said witheringly – although I couldn't help being impressed all the same.

'I've got to try and impress you somehow, haven't I?' he said, digging into my crisps as well as his own. 'I mean, you're hardly likely to be bowled over by my stunning physique, are you?'

'Get out of my crisps! Why do you want to impress me anyway? Just for a free meal ticket?'

He laid his hand on his heart. 'One kick of your long lithe leg and I was literally bowled over. I am now your willing slave, ready to grovel down at your Clarks sensible sandals for all eternity.'

'You are an idiot.'

'Well, at least I'm getting some response out of you. It's

not every bloke who can make a girl laugh *and* cry in the space of ten minutes. What were you crying about anyway?'

'Oh, nothing.'

'That's not a particularly intelligent answer, Sandra.' He leant forward, took hold of his large pink ear and waggled it. 'Whisper into my sympathetic ear.'

'I was just fed up because they wouldn't let me into the Reading Room.'

'Well of course they wouldn't. But why is that such a tragedy?'

'I wanted to find out if my father has ever written a book.'

He paused, nibbling a crisp, his eyebrows wrinkling above the severe frames of his glasses.

'I don't know my father, you see. I'm illegitimate.' I told him as much as I knew myself.

'You mean you've only just asked your mother all this?' he said incredulously.

'Well, I knew a bit. I mean, she's never lied to me or anything. But I never really dared ask her. No, I don't mean dared. I knew she didn't ever want to talk about it and it would be embarrassing and uncomfortable.'

'Like discussing sex with parents?'

'Everything seems to have sexual connotations where you're concerned.'

'That's because I'm obsessively interested in the subject. But don't worry, I'm confining my interest to theory rather than practice for the time being.'

'That's a relief.'

'Anyway, go on about your father.'

'I used to make up all sorts of things about him when I was little but then when I got old enough to understand all the implications, if you see what I mean, I hated him, because he hadn't married my mother and he hadn't wanted anything to do with me. But now I realise it was really his fault. I want to find out more about him, especially now I know he wanted to be a writer.'

'You want to be a writer too, do you?'

'Well. Maybe.' I wasn't so sure, now I hadn't come

anywhere in the competition. 'What do you want to be, Michael? Some sort of professor?'

'Possibly, possibly,' he said, in an elderly eccentric voice, peering over the top of his glasses. Then he twitched his nose to hitch them back into place and drained his coke. 'I like writing too, as a matter of fact. And History and Art. And Human Biology, of course, nudge nudge, wink wink. The Arts subjects. The soft sissy subjects, according to my father. What *I* wouldn't give to be illegitimate! Here, shall I show you my Summer Holiday Project?' He fumbled in his bag and brought out a notebook.

I flicked through it. He'd drawn all sorts of weird grotesque animals and written about them in tiny italic handwriting. I remembered those first-year History lessons.

'It's your own Bestiary,' I said. 'What a good idea.'

He raised his empty coke glass to me, obviously pleased that I knew what a bestiary was.

'It'll have to be my Second Priority Summer Holiday Project now,' he said.

'All right. So what's going to be your Top Priority Summer Holiday Project?'

'Finding your father, of course.'

# Chapter 7

'$B$ᴜᴛ I'm not sure I want to find him,' I said again.

Michael and I were sitting on a bench in Soho Square eating '99' ice-creams.

'You must want to! Out of simple curiosity if nothing else. There's this unknown man wandering around who's given you half your genes, for Heaven's sake.'

'Yes, well I want to find *out* about him. I'd love to read his book, if he ever finished it. I'd love to see what he looks like. But I don't really want to meet him.'

'Are you scared or what?'

'Of course I'm scared. Your infamous intellect's letting you down if you can't work that out for yourself.'

'Sorry. All right, I'm a twit.'

'Anyway, how could I find him?'

'Ask your mother for his address.'

'He's probably moved. That was his parents' house, remember. And I can't ask Mum. I don't want her to know.'

'You know what town he lived in?'

'Yes. Chineford, where my mother lived. It's a little seaside town on the South Coast.'

'Phone up Directory Enquiries and ask them to give you his number.'

'You have to give them an address.'

'Pilbeam isn't a terribly common name. I bet you they'd look it up for you. Come on, we'll go and find a phone box.'

'No! Look, I'll think about it.'

'I'll phone for you if you like.'

'I'm not sure I've got any five pences.'

'Oh Sandra!'

'All right, all right. But what am I going to say supposing there's this very slight chance that he does still live there? I can't just blurt out I'm your long lost daughter. The shock might give him a heart attack or something.'

'Let's just see if we can get the phone number and then we'll work out what you're going to say. Okay?'

I really didn't have any five pence pieces and Michael only had his return ticket home, so he went to a kiosk at Tottenham Court Road tube and bought us a Yorky bar each out of my money, making sure he had plenty of five and ten pences in the change. For a very small, thin boy he seemed to have an enormous appetite.

I was so nervous that even the smell of his chocolate made me feel sick. It was worse in the phone booth, which reeked of stale tobacco and urine.

'The incontinent chain-smoker strikes again,' said Michael, dialling Directory Enquiries for me because my hand had started shaking. My voice went high and squeaky as I asked the operator if she could possibly give me the number of a Mr Pilbeam who lived in Chineford. I half hoped she'd be cross and impatient and tell me she couldn't possibly look it up for me, but she was very helpful.

'Yes, I've found it!' she said, sounding genuinely pleased. 'You're lucky, there's only one Pilbeam. David A. Pilbeam. Is that the right one? The number is. . . .'

I realised I hadn't got a pen or a piece of paper. I tried to memorize the number but I was in such a state that I forgot it the instant she'd said it. I cleared my throat, knowing I should ask her to repeat it, but I stupidly thanked her instead and said goodbye. The receiver was sticky with sweat when I put it down. I stood very still and then I said, giggling stupidly, 'I've only gone and forgotten the number.'

'I haven't.' Michael reeled it off without hesitation and then scrabbled in his bag and wrote it at the back of one of his notebooks.

'I have a remarkable digital memory,' he said. 'It's just as well you bumped into me. Sandra? You're not going to cry again, are you?'

I wasn't sure. I pushed open the door of the phone box and leant against the grimy glass.

'I think I'm going to be sick,' I whispered.

'Oh no,' said Michael. 'Well, there's a wastebin over there. You might as well be neat.'

I hovered uneasily by the waste-bin. It smelt of old sour rubbish which didn't help. After a minute or two I walked shakily back to Soho Square and sat on the same bench. Michael sat beside me. He looked longingly at his half-eaten Yorky but was tactful enough not to bite into it.

'You've gone as white as a sheet,' he said. 'No, to be precise, you're more the colour of natural yoghurt.'

I groaned.

'Sorry, sorry! You're shaking too. You're making the seat wobble.'

'It's just so weird,' I whispered. 'Here I've been, fifteen whole years not having a clue about my father and now in less than five minutes I know exactly where he is. I can ring this number and actually talk to him.'

'Are you going to?'

'I don't know. It's all been too quick and easy. It seems such a silly anticlimax. When adopted people try and trace their mothers, say, they always have weeks and weeks of searching, don't they? It just seems so stupid. I could have rung Directory Enquiries any time. Oh Michael, what am I going to do? Come on, you're the genius. What do you advise?'

'Ring him.'

'And shall I tell him who I am? I *can't*, not on the telephone.'

'Then go and see him. Once you get to Chineford you can look up his address in the local directory. Simple.'

'I haven't got the fare to Chineford for a start.'

'Something tells me you're searching for excuses now.'

'Something tells me it's none of your business anyway,' I said angrily. 'Look, why don't you leave me alone now?'

'I can't, can I? You're suffering from emotional shock. I've got to keep an eye on you.'

'What rubbish. You're just hoping I'll be mug enough to

buy you another ice-cream or a hamburger or whatever.'

'The way to a man's heart is through his stomach.'

'But I don't want to capture your heart, you silly little boy. You obviously have a very high opinion of yourself but I think you're just a pathetic show-off.'

'Spurned!' Michael wailed, making several people turn and stare. He went on making loud, theatrical, sobbing noises. 'Broken!' he gasped, pounding his heart, and then he sank in a heap on the grass.

'Get up, you idiot!' I kicked him gently.

He sat up, grinning at me. 'Come on, let's go and have a browse round Foyles,' he said. 'Let's pretend we've got fifty pounds each, and we'll work out what we're going to spend it on.'

I couldn't help cheering up. It was the sort of game I adored playing, but I'd never found anyone else who liked playing it too. If only Michael was about four or five years older with entirely different looks. Much taller for a start, and not quite so skinny, with a decent casual haircut instead of his ragged short back and sides. It stood up on the crown of his head in a comic little tuft.

'Where on earth do you get your hair cut?' I said, as we walked down Charing Cross Road.

Michael blushed and I wished I hadn't said it.

'My mother cuts it,' he said stiffly.

'Why don't you go to a proper barber's?'

'Because we're hard up, that's why,' he said.

I felt worse than ever, wondering how I could have been so stupid. Had I really thought Michael was wearing his matted hand-knitted jumper, his too-short chain-store jeans, his old plastic bag from choice?

'I'm sorry,' I said humbly. 'Here.' I handed him my unopened Yorky bar.

'We might be poor but we're not actually starving,' he said, chirpy again. He sucked in his cheeks and hunched his shoulders. 'Mamma gives me a bowl of thin gruel every day and sometimes I get a chunk of stale bread too and maybe a morsel of cheese, if Papa hasn't spent every penny on his tankards of ale.'

'Does he drink a lot?'

Michael burst out laughing. 'I was mucking about, you nutcase.'

'Yes, I know, but –'

'No, he doesn't drink. He just doesn't work.'

I wanted to know why, but I'd already put my foot in it enough, so I shut up. Michael broke the Yorky bar in half and we both munched peacefully as we wandered round Foyles. I'd been there once before, but only to the children's department. Michael knew his way round the entire emporium. He chose History books and Art books and a big book on sex with lots of coloured photographs, only neither of us had the nerve to pick it up and have a good look inside it. I chose novels, so I got more books for my fantasy fifty quid, plus a volume of Virginia Woolf's letters and Katherine Mansfield's diary. We were a good hour and a half choosing. It was marvellous being in a good bookshop without Mum nagging at me to get a move on or Julie whining for a wee-wee.

It was gone half-past two by the time we emerged.

'We've missed lunch,' said Michael. 'I'm starving.'

'You can't be serious!'

'No, okay. You've forked out enough on me anyway.'

'What would you have done if I hadn't come along? You haven't got any money.'

He fished in his bag and eventually brought out a very squashed paper bag. He peered inside.

'My Mum's idea of a gourmet feast. A very elderly looking marmite sandwich. Two crumbling cream crackers stuck together with marge. And a very small, withered, yellow apple. Yummy yummy!'

'Don't be rotten. If you're hard up then obviously you can't expect breast of chicken and smoked salmon sandwiches.'

'My Mum would put the mockers on champagne and caviare, I assure you. But help yourself. I should plump for the cream crackers if I were you. This marmite sandwich smells very suspicious.'

We both nibbled tentatively, but ended up in a snack bar

with cups of coffee and large slices of chocolate Swiss roll.

'What cake is dangerous?' Michael asked.

'Mm?'

'Attila the Bun.'

'Okay. What do pixies have for tea?'

'Fairy cakes. Why did the baker stop making doughnuts?'

'Oh no more, Michael, please.'

'Because he got tired of the hole business.'

'You're worse than my little sister. And she's only five.'

'You've got a sister?'

'My mother married when I was eight.'

'So you've got a stepfather?'

I made a face and nodded.

'Wouldn't it be marvellous if we could choose our relations. What sort of parents would you have, Michael?'

'A very young, stylish, classy, rich mother with a fantastic figure who'd done an advanced course in Cordon Bleu cookery.'

'What a male chauvinist piglet choice! And what about your father?'

'I don't think I'd bother with one. What about you?'

'I'd want quite an attractive mother, maybe a bit arty, but I wouldn't want her to be sexy or frivolous. Perhaps she'd be a bit plump, with very short hair, and she'd wear fisherman's smocks and old trousers, and a Liberty print smock and amber beads for best. She'd be very interested in me and encourage me in all my pursuits, but she'd have an important career of her own – maybe she'd write too, or paint, or do sculpture or something – so that she wouldn't be forever hovering over me.'

'I quite like the sound of her too. Is she a good cook?'

'A good plain cook. She makes all her own wholemeal bread and scones and fruitcake and does nourishing vegetarian food, all sorts of quiches and patties and vegetable stews.'

Michael considered. 'I'm not sure I'd like that sort of thing.'

'Well, she's not your pretend mother, she's mine.'

'And your father?'

'He doesn't really match her, because he's younger and more elegant, very witty and intellectual, but he's sensitive too. He looks fabulous in beautifully cut suits and expensive pastel shirts but he's really happiest in Guernsey sweaters and comfy old cords. He's very knowledgeable, and he takes me round museums and art galleries and explains everything and makes it interesting, and sometimes we go to French and Italian restaurants together after we've been to a play or a film. That's while we're in London. He's also got a cottage in the countryside. No, maybe it's by the sea, I'm not quite sure yet. It's on the top of a cliff overlooking the sea, *and* it's the countryside too, and we go for marvellous long bracing walks, sometimes across the cliff-tops and deep into the woods, other times along the sea-shore, scrabbling over the rocks. And then in the evenings we sit in front of a log fire and roast chestnuts and he reads aloud to me or else we play classical music. . . .'

'And he writes novels and when he's not living in his London flat and his cliff-top cottage he lives in Chineford?' said Michael.

I started to feel sick again. I didn't reply. Michael took out his notebook and tore out the last page, with my father's telephone number in his neat handwriting. He handed it to me and I carefully folded the paper until it was a minute hard square and put it in my purse.

'Are you going to phone now?'

'No.' I looked at my watch. 'I think I'd better go home.'

Michael looked shocked. 'But it's only the middle of the afternoon! What a waste of train fare. What time did you say you'd be back?'

'I didn't. But I suppose Mum expects me back for tea about sixish.'

'Where do you live?'

'Kingtown.'

'That's not all that far from me. I live in Blyton Park. Great, we can go home on the same train. But we've got ages yet. Which do you like best, the National Gallery or the Portrait Gallery? Or are you in an ecclesiastical mood? We could do a few churches if you like, or else we could switch from saints to sinners and potter round the sex spots of Soho.'

'You choose,' I said, not wanting to admit that I'd never been to any of them.

Michael plumped for Soho and so we set off down Old Compton Street. I was amazed by the sex shops. The things they had in the windows! Satin bras and knickers with holes in the rudest places, huge false you-know-whats and all sorts of weird devices that I'd never even heard of. I didn't know what they were for and I don't think Michael did either, although he pretended he did. He said there were even more outlandish things inside and assured me that it was perfectly okay for us to go and have a look round, in spite of the notices on the door of every sex shop saying you had to be over eighteen to come in. So I dared him and he hesitated for five minutes and then suddenly went rushing in. He shot out again after a few seconds but I suppose he won the dare. I let him think he had anyway.

He said he was beginning to find the sex shops a bit boring so we went down to the Portrait Gallery and spent a long time deliberating on the three historical figures we'd most like to have been. I chose Charlotte Brontë, Elizabeth Barratt Browning and Virginia Woolf.

'An interesting but rather sickly trio,' said Michael. 'You obviously don't mind the thought of languishing on a chaise longue or going periodically dotty.'

He chose Shakespeare, William Morris and George Eliot.

'But George Eliot's a woman,' I protested.

'So what? There's no sexist discrimination in my pretend games, thank you very much. She's a much more interesting literary lady than your lot because she's very intellectual *and* very passionate *and* she doesn't give a damn about convention *and* she was healthy to boot.'

I peered at her portrait.

'But she wasn't very pretty,' I said.

'Now who's acting like a male chauvinist pig?' Michael said, laughing at me.

I bought picture postcard reproductions of all six in the shop downstairs and on the train going home, when we were nearly at Blyton Park, I pressed Shakespeare, William Morris and George Eliot into Michael's hand.

'It's been a smashing day. Thanks for showing me round everywhere, Michael – and for helping me find that phone number. I hope you get your bestiary finished. I'll look out for you if I ever go to the British Museum again.' I'd been rehearsing my little speech in my head ever since we left Waterloo.

Michael looked at me as if I was mad.

'What are you on about? We'll be going to the British Museum together, well, when I can afford the fare. And I've been trying to think of a good meeting place half-way between Blyton Park and Kingtown. It's obviously Mallington, so we'd better meet outside Mallington Town Hall.' The train slowed down and drew into Blyton Park station. 'See you there at ten o'clock tomorrow. Take a packed lunch. I hope your Mum's better at it than mine. See you.'

He got off the train and was gone before I could reply.

# Chapter 8

*I* MET Michael nearly every day that summer holiday. Mum looked worried when I told her I'd met a boy in London and wanted to go on seeing him.

'I don't know, Sandra. I mean, there are limits. I don't like the idea at all, you being picked up on the street.'

'It wasn't on the street, for a start. It was in the British Museum,' I said grandly.

'What on earth were you there for?'

'Because I wanted to have a look round. We're not all cultural morons in this family.'

'Hey, hey! Now don't start, Madam. Did you go and look at the mummies then?' I could tell she was pleased she knew about the mummies at the museum.

'No, I didn't actually. I spent most of my time in the manuscript rooms. That's where I met Michael. He's doing a bestiary as a Summer Holiday Project. A bestiary's a book about imaginary animals and birds.'

'So he's a schoolboy,' said Mum, looking amused and relieved.

Her attitude irritated me. I knew she'd look even more amused and relieved if she had actually seen Michael.

'Well, yes, but he's in the sixth form,' I lied. I told her the real school Michael went to and she raised her eyebrows.

'That's a public school, isn't it? His parents can't be short of a bob or two then.'

Michael had won a scholarship but I knew Mum would be more impressed by money than brains.

I invented a very rich executive father for Michael and I

gave him his own fantasy mother, the classy Cordon Bleu cook.

'You've met them, then?'

'Yes, we had afternoon tea at Michael's home. They live in this huge, rambling Victorian house overlooking Mallington Common.'

'What did they give you for tea then?'

I invented a feast that would have even satisfied Michael. Perhaps I overdid it because Mum looked at me suspiciously.

'Smoked salmon sandwiches? Don't you mean tinned?'

'Smoked, but they weren't very nice actually. I think they'd been in the fridge because the bread was a bit cold and tasteless,' I said quickly, trying to add authentic detail. 'And one of the cakes was stale, only of course I didn't say anything.'

'I suppose they put on a huge spread just to show off,' Mum said, more happily. 'And you're meeting this Michael again today? Oh dear, I suppose it's our turn to provide the tea.'

'Oh no,' I said hastily. 'No, it's all right, Mum, really. I don't think we're going to bother with tea today. We're having a picnic lunch. Can I make myself some sandwiches?'

'Well, we haven't got any smoked salmon. You'll have to make do with Dairylea or liver sausage,' said Mum. She hesitated. 'Look, lovie, don't think I'm not pleased for you that you've found a friend, but you're still very young. You will be sensible, won't you?'

'Of course.'

'You know what I mean, don't you?'

'Yes!'

'It's just – well, I can remember the way I felt when I met . . . your father. I was pretty bowled over by him, Sandra. He wasn't as well off as this Michael sounds, but he led a different kind of life from me and I thought he was the bee's knees. I forgot myself, Sandra, lost all my common sense.'

'Well, I won't.'

'Yes, but you've no idea how difficult it can be,' Mum said anxiously. 'And boys like that can be very callous about girls who aren't quite from the same background. They're often only after one thing, you know.'

I sighed. Mum looked at me carefully. Then she frowned. I certainly didn't look much of a sex object. I'd managed to talk her into buying me a pair of dungarees at last. They were very baggy indeed. I was wearing a faded Puffin T-shirt underneath and my old school sandals.

'You were with Kim when you met Michael?' she said thoughtfully.

She was too tactful to say it but 'WHY ON EARTH DID HE PICK SANDRA WHEN HE COULD HAVE HAD KIM?' was written all over her face. I thought hard.

'I know Kim's much prettier than me but I think her sort of girl frightens Michael. He's very quiet and shy. He's not used to girls at all, because he hasn't got any sisters and he goes to this posh boys' school.'

'Ah. I see,' said Mum. 'Mind you, these shy silent types are often the worst.' But she was joking, convinced now that this lordly young man looked on me as a sweet little surrogate sister.

She asked me several times in the following weeks to invite Michael back home, but was oddly understanding when I hedged and made excuses.

'I think we ought to have a deck at this bloke,' I heard Stan grumble in their bedroom. 'Especially after all that to-do the last time she got herself a boy.'

'That was different, love. And I think we were a bit hard on her anyway. Still, that's all water under the bridge. This boy sounds a different type altogether. Sandra's really bettered herself with this one. And I don't think there's anything serious about the relationship. I mean, he's quite a bit older than her, and Sandra's young for her age in lots of ways. It's just a friendship, Stan, and I'm really pleased. It's made all the difference in the world to her. There haven't been any moods or sulks for ages.'

Mum was right about it making a difference, although hearing her say it like that was irritating. I'd never had a friend like Michael. Even in the old days with Kim I'd always put on a bit of an act with her, never quite daring to tell her what I really thought. But I didn't have to think twice with Michael. I could come out with the weirdest things and he never once laughed or scoffed or tapped his forehead and told me I was nuts. He had some pretty weird ideas of his own. Best of all, we sometimes found we'd both had the *same* weird ideas.

Ever since I'd read about the Brontë children I'd been fascinated by imaginary Angria and Gondal worlds and I'd made up several lands of my own, with little books and drawings and a miniature newspaper. It turned out Michael had been doing this for years, on an even more elaborate scale, with tiny models and huge maps and the journals of all his main characters. We started making up a new land together called Michaelandra, for obvious reasons. One day we tried acting it out as we wandered over Mallington common, but we were stiff and self-conscious, and the imagining never became vivid and real, the way it does when you're little. So most of the time we sat in quiet copses with our notebooks and pencils and felt tips, swopping ideas and writing it all out. Michael's ideas were generally more inventive than mine, but I could write better ballads than he could, and my drawings of people were better too, although his castles and mythical creatures were superb.

When it rained we went round the shops and museums and churches and libraries in Mallington, Kingtown, Blyton Park and surrounding district. I never suggested we went back to my house and Michael never suggested we went back to his.

At first Michael asked me every day if I'd phoned my father and nagged me about it, but after a while he stopped mentioning him. Perhaps he was being tactful, perhaps he'd simply forgotten about it.

I certainly hadn't forgotten. I'd started dreaming about my father every night. Not dreams, nightmares. I was lost in dark forests or struggling in stagnant water, screaming for someone who never came. I'd wake up sweating and be so scared that I wanted to rush to Mum and cuddle in beside her, like Julie. I didn't need a psychiatrist to help me figure out the meaning of my dreams.

I still had the phone number, wrapped up tightly in my purse. I took it out nearly every day and held it in my clenched fist, trying to pluck up the courage to phone. The rare times I was alone in the house the telephone in the hall seemed to grow monstrously, its squat toad shape swelling until it pressed against the walls and ceiling and there was no way I could ignore its presence. Sometimes I knelt in front of it, trembling, dialled one digit, and then slammed the receiver down. One day I sat for half an hour, rocking backwards and forwards, biting my lips, and then I dialled the whole number but I threw the receiver down in terror when I heard the first ring.

The next day, catching the train to Mallington to meet Michael as usual, I asked the booking-clerk the price of a return half-fare to Chineford. (The only times I was glad I looked so young for my age were when I was travelling.) It was £7.10. Not really very much. Mum gave me a couple of pounds every few days, to help out with fares and snacks, and Stan often gave me money too. I could try saving it all up or earn some money of my own.

Michael made me feel ashamed, because he took it for granted that he earned his own pocket-money, getting up at six every morning to do a newspaper round. He saved one pound a week towards books, gave another pound to his mother, and kept £1.50 for his own fares and food. He let me treat him to cokes and coffees and chocolate, but never anything but food. The one time we went out together in the evening to see a film he insisted on paying for both tickets, although they were £1.80 each. (This time we were trying hard to look old for our age, because it was an AA.)

It felt strange being in the cinema with Michael. Somehow I couldn't relax. I was very conscious of everyone round us, knowing we looked very small and skinny and silly together, our glasses glinting in the semi-darkness. I was worried that Michael might try to put his arm round me or kiss me. We had talked about sex in extraordinarily intimate terms, both of us getting very hot and red although we struggled to stay cool and casual, but we'd never so much as held hands. I wanted it to stay that way. Michael was a friend who happened to be a boy, that was all. *Not* a boy-friend. How could he possibly be my boy-friend when he was eighteen months younger than me and so funny looking?

Now we were really used to each other he didn't try to chat me up the way he'd done in the British Museum. In fact he'd become quite reticent about his feelings, but I was pretty sure he still liked me. Liked me a lot.

Every time he stretched or shifted his position I tensed, wondering what to do, but he didn't even put his arm on the back of my seat, let alone round my shoulders. It was a relief – and yet I was obscurely disappointed too. If he really liked me then why didn't he try to kiss me?

He came out of the cinema starving as usual and bought us both a bag of fish and chips which we ate on the way to Mallington Station.

'At least let me pay for the fish and chips, Michael. I told you, Stan gave me a five pound note the other day.'

'No, it's my treat for once. *I* got a fiver this morning too.'

'How come?'

'One of my readers' letters. Mine was the star letter, so I got five quid instead of two.'

'You wrote a letter to a paper?'

'A women's magazine. I was Mrs A., Harrow, writing about my cute grandchildren. Little Johnnie's nauseating utterances in the local launderette, and then I popped in a handy washing hint as well.'

I burst out laughing.

'You can laugh. Last year I bought a fountain pen, a handful of Penguins and my entire, ghastly, school games-kit out of my writing profits.'

'But which magazine do you write to?'

'All of them. I have a different name and personality for each one, only I always have to give my own address of course, for when the cheque comes. You want to have a go yourself, Sandra, it's ever so easy. Try some of the teenage magazines. I should think half their readers can't write an intelligible sentence so they're thrilled with the most banal letter. I'm Lorraine T. who's ever so good at making collages

67

out of her pop pics from her fave mag, and I'm Sharon N. who keeps making silly boobs and ends all her letters, "Honestly, I could've died!!!" She always puts three exclamation marks, but all of them pepper their pages with zany punctuation. Oh, and they all have different handwriting too. I don't suppose it's necessary, because I shouldn't think there's much liason between the magazines, but it's fun making up different writing styles. I've got a very rigid copperplate that belongs to this frightful 15-year-old twit Alexander Gibbons-Green who writes to the Junior Letters page in the Daily Mail. He thinks we should bring back National Service and put all sexual offenders in stocks and pelt them with rotten eggs.'

'But couldn't you get into trouble if anyone ever found out? It's fraud, isn't it?'

'Possibly. But I shouldn't imagine the magazines would ever make a fuss about it. If I didn't keep sending them good copy then one of their junior sub-editors would have to sit down each week and fill up the gaps in their letters pages. And half the magazines are semi-fraudulent themselves. What about the confession ones, where it's all meant to be true?'

'And they're not true at all?'

'Oh Sandra! Grow up! As if the sort of heroines supposedly writing the stories would be able to write it all in that breathy melodramatic manner, carrying on for four or five thousand words? I thought I might have a bash at one of them myself, I bet they pay really well. In fact they have some from the man's point of view. Yes, I'll be poor wretched Mike, passionate about sexy Sandra, only she's having a tempestuous affair with. . . . Who do you want to be having it off with, eh?'

I threw my empty chip-bag at him.

'No-one, you nutcase. Here Michael, can you lend me some old copies of these magazines? I think I'll have a bash at some readers' letters too.'

I thought they'd be simple to write, but I found I didn't have Michael's knack at all. It took me ages to think of something to write about, and then I spun it out for far too long so that it was more of a short story than a letter. I sent off ten and none of them got chosen for publication.

But something else did. I noticed that some of the teenage magazines had proper short stories, as well as picture strips and confessions. I had a copy of my Rosamund competition story. I dug it out and sent it off to one of the magazines without telling anyone. I got a letter back from the magazine a fortnight later.

> 'Dear Sandra,
>     Thanks for sending us DADDY'S GIRL. It's a great little story although it needs a bit of work on it. Don't worry, we'll do that this end. Our cheque for £20 for all rights will be on its way to you soon. We'd like to see some more of your work.
>                     Cheers!'

This time I read the letter through carefully twice before telling Mum and Stan. They were very nice about it. And Julie put her arms round me and gave me a hug, which made me feel very guilty indeed. It's awful when your five-year-old sister proves herself to be a much nicer person than you are yourself.

Stan even offered me a celebration meal too but I tactfully refused.

'But I tell you what would be wonderful, Stan,' I said, laying on the sweetness and charm. 'You wouldn't lend me the £20 now, would you? Then I could have some spending money while I'm still on holiday. I'll give you the cheque as soon as it comes, I promise.'

Mum looked a bit doubtful, but Stan put his hand in his wallet straight away and produced four five pound notes with a flourish.

'I don't like you having all that money at once, Sandra. You're not going to waste it, are you? What are you going to buy? Have you seen a dress you like or what?' Mum asked.

'I'd like to use some of it to have a lovely day out with Michael,' I said. 'I want to treat him for a change.'

'Yes, that's a good idea,' Mum said, relieved. 'Where do

you plan to go? How about the seaside, if this lovely weather holds?'

'Yes, that's what I thought,' I said. 'Next Saturday.'

# Chapter 9

*I* FELT fine for most of the journey, reading my book and playing silly pencil and paper games with Michael, but when we started getting near Chineford my throat dried and my tummy turned to jelly. I had to trek along to the smelly little lavatory at the end of the corridor and yet I needed to go again as soon as I stepped onto the station platform. Michael browsed at the bookstall while I went in search of a Ladies. There was a telephone inside the waiting room, with a local directory. I fumbled through the pages to the P's. The operator was right, there was just the one Pilbeam. David A. Pilbeam, 31 Netherfield Way, Chineford. I wrote it down and then folded that piece of paper very small too and put it in my purse.

Michael was waiting outside the Ladies when I eventually came out.

'Are you okay?'

'Well. Sort of.'

'You don't look it. Come on. You'd better get some sea air.'

We marched resolutely down the hill towards the sea. It had been bright and sunny at home, but it was very overcast here, and a strong wind blew as we got nearer the beach. I'd taken a lot of care with my clothes. It wasn't the sort of day for dungarees. I'd shortened my long Laura Ashley dress. I hoped it looked a lot better at its new calf length. It didn't go with my denim jacket so I'd taken a chance that I'd be warm enough without it. Only I wasn't.

'You're shivering,' said Michael.

'My, aren't we observant,' I snapped, rubbing my bare

blue arms and tucking my chin into my chest against the wind.

'Do you want to borrow my sweater?'

It was sweet of him, but I snapped again.

'I can hardly wear your scarlet sweater over a pink dress. Honestly!'

'All right then, stay shivering,' said Michael.

We walked along the front in silence. I ignored the grey sea and dun sands to my left and the ice-cream stalls and gaudy amusement arcades to my right, concentrating fiercely on the salmon paving stones underfoot. I played the not walking on any cracks game.

'What happens if you manage it?' Michael said, guessing what I was doing.

I shrugged, not wanting to talk to him.

'Look, why don't you get it over and done with?' said Michael. 'Your father lives at 31 Netherfield Way.'

'How the hell do you know?' I said furiously.

'Because I looked it up in the station when you were being such ages in the toilet.'

'Lavatory. I can't stick people who say toilet.'

'I can think of far worse words for it than toilet,' said Michael, and started to chant his way through a long offensive list.

'Do shut *up*.'

'All right. Netherfield Way is up on that hilly part there. I asked the woman at the newspaper stall. It's the posh part of Chineford. Don't worry, Sandra, I'm sure the dreaded word toilet has never issued forth from your father's upper-class lips.'

'Can't you just shut up altogether?' I walked rapidly away from him towards the pier. I paid five pence, pushed through the creaking turnstile, and stalked up the pier. I stared at the wooden planks. I could see the churning sea through the gaps. It was so cold I could hardly get my breath. My hair whipped my face and I had to clutch my skirt.

'Sandra!' Michael came running after me. 'I know your sense of direction is poor, but surely even you realise Netherfield Way is not at the end of the pier.'

'All *right*. I'm not going there.'

'So okay, you're not going there. We've come all this way and wasted all that money for nothing.'

'I just wanted a day out, that's all.'

'So what are you going to do?'

'Walk. Look around. Go on the beach.'

'It's blowing a bloody gale.'

'I don't care. Oh for Heaven's sake, Michael, leave me alone. Stop asking your stupid questions. You make me sick.'

'Then why did you want me to come?'

'I don't know. I wish I hadn't asked you. I wish I hadn't come myself.'

I started running. The old planks were wet with spray and I nearly slipped but I ran even faster, blood rushing painfully to my numb feet. I ran past the Bingo Hall, the Hot Do-nut stand and the Ice-cream Parlour, the Mini Bowl and Madame Rose, Fortune Teller, past the Chineford Pier Theatre, past patient fishermen and pensioners hunched under plaid rugs, right to the very end of the pier. I only slowed down at the last moment, banging my chest painfully against the rusty railing. I leant against the cold bars and put my head in my hands.

I heard the thud of Michael's trainers, petering out as he panted up beside me. He said nothing. I kept my head bowed. I felt something warm go round my shoulder and saw familiar scarlet wool through a crack in my fingers. Michael had his arm round me.

'I'm sorry I was so hateful,' I mumbled.

'It's okay,' said Michael, awkwardly patting my back. 'You didn't half give me a fright though. I thought you were going to go on running right into the sea.'

'Not me,' I said, straightening up. Michael took his arm away at once. I managed a smile. 'I'm too much of a coward to go and look up David Pilbeam.'

'Oh well. It doesn't matter. He's probably not that thrilling anyway. You're right, we'll just have a nice day out.'

It was spitting with rain and we were both shivering.

'We couldn't have picked a better day,' I said, and started laughing.

73

Michael laughed too.

'I'm starving. All this emotional trauma does wonders for my appetite. Let's see what delicacies my Mum has come up with this time. I fear the ubiquitous marmite. She must have shares in the company.'

He delved in his airline bag. 'Here, she's put in another jumper. My school one. Navy blue. Does that go with pink?'

It didn't, but I took it gratefully and put it on.

'It's a bit worn round the elbows. And hang on, I think there's a streak of school custard down the front,' Michael said worriedly.

'Who cares,' I said. 'Thanks, Michael.'

I knew I must look a sight. The wind had tangled my hair, Michael's sweater was shabby, my Laura Ashley dress looked like a long dress hastily turned up rather than a new short dress, and my best blue suede sandals were blackening with damp, but for once I truly didn't care.

We walked back along the pier and I bought us each a hot Do-nut and a strawberry ice-cream and then we walked into the town and had fish and chips and a plate of bread and butter and a cup of tea in the Deep Sea Restaurant. It was raining quite hard when we came out of the restaurant so we looked for a cinema, but the only one we could find was showing a second-rate Walt Disney, so we gave it a miss. We walked round the shopping centre instead. Michael got a bit fidgety when I looked in dress shops, but we spent half an hour in a tiny W. H. Smith's and had another long browse in a truly awful souvenir emporium.

'Ooh Sandra, what present would you like, dear heart? How about this delightful plastic Venus de Milo surrounded by artificial flowers? Or a corkscrew with this cute little boy having a widdle? No wait, here we are, the perfect gift.' He pounced on an ashtray in the shape of a miniature lavatory. 'A dinky little *toilet*!'

We both shrieked with laughter and the middle-aged sales assistant was so affronted she told us to get out of the shop if we weren't going to buy anything.

I got out of the shop straight away but Michael lingered

mysteriously. He came out a few minutes later with a paper bag in his hand.

'You bought something! For your Mum?'

'Of course not. For you.'

I thought it was a joke and that it was probably the toilet ashtray so I got ready to laugh, but it was a tiny mouse made out of shells, with a dainty little face and a long pink cord tail.

'Oh Michael, she's lovely! You shouldn't have. But I'm so glad you did. I didn't even notice any mice in the shop. Oh thank you, thank you ever so much.' I bobbed my head forward and kissed his cheek. It felt very smooth and soft. We both blushed.

'Note the pink tail. To match your dress,' said Michael.

'I'm going to call her Michaela Mouse, after you. But what can I get you? Hey, I'll have to go back into that shop!'

'I'm not sentimental like you. I'd sooner you went into a sweet-shop. Hint hint.'

I ignored all the little newsagents and kiosks and waited until I found a proper old-fashioned sweet-shop, and then I bought Michael a quarter of all the more expensive sweets, buttered brazils and maple walnuts, cherry fudge and chocolate dates, rose and violet creams and raspberry nougat.

He seemed delighted and crammed his mouth full before remembering the way I'd thanked him.

'Come here. It's my turn to kiss you.'

'You've got chocolate all round your mouth. No thanks!'

There was a large toy shop nearby and we went in there to have a nostalgic look round. There were several packets of Cindy dresses that Julie hadn't got, and I wondered about buying her a present, but I'd already bought some sticks of rock in the sweet-shop and decided that they would do instead. Julie had far too many toys anyway. I'd only had one doll and one teddy for most of my childhood and I'd managed all right. No, two dolls.

'Hey, I bet this was the shop my grandma took me to, when I was staying with her. She bought me a baby doll and then got all narked with me because her arm came off.'

'Your gran lives here still?'

'No! She died.'

75

'Do you remember where she lived?'

'Not really. I only came here once, just for the week-end. She didn't seem like my real grandma if you see what I mean. I've always felt hard done by, not having any doting grans.'

'Maybe you've still got one.'

'What do you mean?'

'David Pilbeam's mother.'

'Yes, of course. How weird. I know it's mad, but it didn't really dawn on me. I wonder what she's like? I didn't like the sound of her, not from what my Mum said, although I don't think she actually met her. Mum thought they were very snobby. So I suppose David Pilbeam will be too. Michael . . . shall we just go and see what his house is like? See if it's a really big one?'

'Come on then.'

It was a moderately big house, a sturdy nineteen-thirties detached villa, pebble-dashed and painted pale pink.

'To match your dress,' said Michael.

I managed a smile although my tummy was churning again. I looked up at each window in turn. There wasn't a sign of anyone. I wondered which was his bedroom window. The front window probably, with the Sanderson flowers, very tasteful. I scrutinised the other curtains. Nothing garish or girlish. I peered at the garden: it was surprisingly neglected, although someone had recently cut the privet and grass. Weeds straggled beneath unpruned rose-bushes in the flower beds. No tennis balls, no plastic tea-sets or miniature cars abandoned on the crazy paving. No sand-pits or bikes or skateboards.

'It doesn't look as if he's got any children,' I said. 'Well, as far as one can tell.'

I waited anxiously for Michael to agree with me.

'What about a wife, Miss Holmes?'

'Oh, I expect he's got a wife. Who would probably object pretty strongly to me, so I can't just barge in and say, "Hello Daddy".'

'I see your point.'

We both stood watching the house. It looked very still and silent. The man in number 29 was out cleaning his car. A woman in number 33 was kneeling on a cushion, weeding.

'She's putting David Pilbeam to shame,' I said. 'His garden's a bit of a mess. Of course, if he's a writer he's probably a bit scruffy and eccentric and doesn't mind a few weeds.'

But it didn't look as if that sort of person lived there at all. It was such a conventional, conservative house. A house for a businessman or bank manager. Only it had grown old and seedy. It wasn't just the unkempt garden. The pale pink paint was peeling, the edge of one window sill had crumbled away, and the ornamental iron gate had rusted badly.

'Perhaps he's fallen on hard times. After all, none of his books are now in print. Maybe he's suffering from a terrible case of writer's block.'

'So go and find out.'

'I can't, I told you. His wife will be there.'

'It doesn't look as if anyone's there, if you ask me,' said Michael. 'All the windows are shut, look.'

'Oh no,' I said, although I was relieved. 'I deliberately picked a Saturday, thinking that was the best time to find him in. If he's not a writer then he'll obviously be out at work during the week. People don't work on Saturdays, do they?'

'Some do.'

'Still, if he's definitely out I could ring just to make sure and then maybe have a peer in the downstairs windows. I'd like to see what sort of furniture he's got. But what shall I say if there is somebody in after all? What if his wife comes to the door?'

'Say you're collecting for something.'

'I haven't got a box.'

'I know, pretend you're going to do a sponsored walk. Hang on, I'll make you out a sheet of paper and shove a few signatures down, to make it look authentic.' Michael got busy, balancing on one leg so that he could rest the paper on his other knee.

'You will come with me, won't you?' I begged him.

'All right. If you want me to.'

'Of course I do!'

'What if Daddy comes to the door though? Shall I lurk in the shrubbery whilst the grand reunion takes place?'

'No, you stick to me.'

Michael looked pleased.

'Right you are.'

He handed me my forged sponsorship form and gave my hand a quick squeeze. Then we walked together up the path to the door of number 31. Flakes of rust from the gate stuck to my sweaty hand. Michael reached up to rap the knocker, but I suddenly remembered I looked a real sight. It had stopped raining so I took off Michael's school sweater and tried to smooth my creased dress. I dragged a comb through my tangled hair and mopped at my muddy shoes with a tissue.

'Come on. You look fine,' Michael lied gallantly.

He knocked and I held my breath. Nothing at all happened. Michael knocked again. My heart thudded. We waited.

'Talk about an anti-climax. You're right, nobody's in,' I said shakily – but just as I finished speaking the door opened.

# *Chapter 10*

'*Y*ES?' A middle-aged woman in a flowery nylon overall stood looking at us enquiringly. She was very fat but
firmly corsetted, so that the only flesh free to wobble was on
her large, mottled arms. She folded them and waited.

I forgot all about pretending to be on a sponsored walk.

'I'm very sorry to bother you, but are you Mrs Pilbeam?' I
said.

'Good heavens no, duck,' she said, surprised. 'No, dear,
Mrs Pilbeam passed over two years ago now.'

'She's dead?'

She nodded and sighed. 'Very sad.'

'What about Mr Pilbeam? Mr David Pilbeam?'

'What about him, dear?'

'Does he still live here?'

'Oh yes. Although. . . .' She hesitated and didn't continue.

'Is he in now?'

'Of course he's in.'

'Then could I possibly see him?'

She looked doubtful. I smoothed my hair again and looked
at her pleadingly.

'Well, I don't know,' she said. 'You know he's not very
well, don't you?'

'No, I didn't know. Is it anything serious?'

'Well, you could say that, I suppose.'

'Please let me see him, just for a minute. I've come a very
long way. I used to know him, a long time ago.'

'All right then. Just for a minute or two. Although I'm not
sure there's really much point. Still, I don't suppose it will do
any harm. Come along in, both of you.'

'I'll stay here,' said Michael when we were in the hall, but I grabbed his hand.

'No, please come with me, Michael, please.'

So he came too.

The fat woman paused at a closed door.

'We've put him down here in the sitting-room for now. It's best, really. In you come then.'

She ushered us into the room. An awful smell hung heavily in the air, thick and sour and stale. One wall had French windows leading out onto the back garden but they were closed. An ugly electric fire stood in the old tiled fireplace, both bars full on. The heat made the smell worse. A row of medicine bottles and pills and tonic wine had taken over as ornaments on the mantlepiece, and several hot-water bottles and musty blankets were scattered across the stained carpet. The large bed took up most of the room. An old man was lying under the covers at a lopsided angle. His mouth hung open and a dribble of saliva trickled down his whiskery chin. He breathed heavily, as if he were asleep, but his eyes were open. He stared blankly at Michael and me.

I couldn't say anything. Michael eventually cleared his throat and mumbled, 'Good afternoon, Sir.'

The man in the bed grunted something unintelligible.

'I'm sorry?' said Michael.

'It's all right, dear, he's only talking nonsense. Just babbling like a baby. He's been like that ever since the second stroke this spring. Left him helpless. He's got no control, you know. None at all. I have to change him, and it's not very nice, I can tell you.'

I stared in agony at the man, wondering if he could understand what she was saying. For a moment he seemed to be looking straight at me and my stomach clenched in pity and fear, but then his yellowy eyes moved on and he stared fixedly at nothing at all.

'How old is he?' I whispered.

'Mm? How old, dear? I couldn't rightly say. Not a very great age. Late sixties, I suppose. He aged badly after Mrs Pilbeam passed over. It came as such a shock, you see. She went into hospital for a simple little gall-bladder operation and couldn't withstand the anaesthetic. Snuffed out like a candle, there on the operating table.'

My cheek muscles twitched and I bit the insides of my mouth to stop myself snorting with inappropriate laughter.

'Mr and Mrs Pilbeam have a son, don't they?' said Michael.

'That's right, dear. And a daughter too.'

'I think we've made a silly mistake. I think it's this Mr Pilbeam's son that my friend knows.'

'Mm? Oh, I see.'

'They both have the same Christian name, David?' said Michael. 'That's how we got mixed up.'

'But the younger Mr Pilbeam hasn't lived here for donkey's years, since he went away to college,' she said. 'I thought you said you knew him, dear?' She looked at me.

'Yes, but I – I was very little. I've obviously got mixed up.'

'Oh well. No harm done.'

The man in the bed grunted again, his mouth opening and shutting fruitlessly.

'What does he want?' I whispered.

'Search me. He doesn't know what he's doing, dear.' She turned to the man and spoke to him as if he were a naughty toddler. 'Now you stop that silly noise, you're frightening this young lady.'

'No, no, it's all right,' I said.

I knew I ought to try to make some sort of effort for the poor man in the bed. He was my grandfather, preposterous though it seemed. I ought to tell the fat woman to go away. I could sit by his side and hold his hand and show him I wasn't frightened. But I was frightened, and although I hated the fat woman and her mouthful of stupid platitudes I was glad she was there, protecting me from the pitiful grunts of the old man.

He went on grunting, sounding like an animal. I didn't want to look at him but I couldn't help it. I was horrified to see tears on his sallow cheeks.

'He's crying,' I whispered.

'No, he's not, dear, his eyes just get watery,' said the fat woman. She took a tissue from a box of Kleenex and dabbed at his face without tenderness. 'There. Dry those old eyes, eh?'

He went on grunting while we stood staring at him. I tried desperately to think of something to say. At last I mumbled inadequately, 'Well, I suppose we'd better be going.' I turned to the bed and said, 'Goodbye. I hope you get better soon.'

'Oh no, dear, there's no recovering, not when they've got to this stage,' said the fat woman. 'He's just a vegetable now.'

I wanted to hit her for saying it in front of him, even if he really couldn't understand.

Michael had far more courage.

'That's not informed medical opinion, that's only your own supposition,' he said, but politely. 'And as a matter of fact, there is a current scientific school of thought that believes even vegetables have some sort of feelings.' He went over to the man in the bed and took his hand. 'Goodbye, Sir. I'm sorry if we tired you. Would you like me to plump up your pillows for you?'

The grunt could have meant anything but Michael chose to interpret it as yes. He carefully eased the frail old man forwards and then expertly rearranged the three pillows. 'There. I hope that's more comfortable,' he said, helping him lie back.

The old man really did look more comfortable. He went on grunting, but he didn't sound quite so agonised. We went out of the room and the fat woman closed the door. I could still smell the thick sour invalid smell. It seemed to be clogging my nostrils.

'You're a quaint little kid,' the fat woman said to Michael, not seeming to bear him any grudge. 'I could do with you living here, to give me a hand. You've got quite a way with old Mr Pilbeam, haven't you?'

Michael ignored the compliment. 'You don't happen to know Mr Pilbeam's son's address, do you?'

'Yes dear. Don't I just. I'm going to have to get in touch with him again, that's for certain. I've been lumbered, there's no doubt about it. Will you two be going to see him?

Because you tell him that it's just not good enough. You tell him Mrs Alcott has had enough and he'll have to look after his father himself or get him into a home or whatever. It's not my responsibility. I just came in to do for Mrs Pilbeam, that's the way it started, and that's the way it should have been kept. When the poor soul passed over Mr Pilbeam begged me to come as a living-in housekeeper and it wasn't really what I wanted at all. I should have kept my own little flat and let him get on with it. But I've too soft a heart for my own good, and that's a fact. I gave up my flat, I gave up my other cleaning jobs, I gave up my friends. I came here and I looked after Mr Pilbeam and I kept this big house looking lovely and cooked three good meals a day, and when he had his first stroke I even took on a bit of nursing, just out of the kindness of my heart. He went to stay with Susan, she's the daughter, but she couldn't get rid of him quick enough, scared she was going to be lumbered for good. Then she ups and goes to the U.S. of A. if you please, so she's not even on hand when his Lordship has his second stroke. *I'm* the one that's lumbered, oh yes. But I can't go on. It's too much to ask of anyone. I'm sorry for the poor old boy, but it's not as if he's my own flesh and blood, now is it? Well, is it?' She looked at us for some sort of answer.

'Doesn't Mr Pilbeam – the younger one – doesn't he even come to visit his father?' I said.

'Once in a blue moon, if that. No, it's not good enough. Last time I had a little grumble he just offered me more money, but that's not what I want. I can't be bought. I want my freedom, that's what I want. It's not my responsibility.' She whined relentlessly, like a dentist's drill.

'I'm afraid we've got to catch a train very shortly,' Michael interrupted at last. 'So could we have the younger Mr Pilbeam's address?'

She went into another room leading off the hall. It was a study, with a big desk and several bookcases. I wanted to wander round, having a proper look, but she scribbled the address on the back of an old postcard in seconds.

'Here we are then. And you say you'll go and see him? It's a long way away mind.'

I stared at the address. My father lived in Lychmond. It was the other side of London, about twelve miles from Kingtown. Not really that far away at all.

'Yes, I'll go and see him,' I said. 'I wonder – is he married?'

She frowned at me.

'What, dear? Of course he's married, and he's got the two kiddies, but that doesn't mean to say he can palm his own father off on a stranger, now does it? I know he's got commitments to his own family but his father's his family too, isn't he? I'm still not quite clear. How exactly do you know him, dear?'

'It's – it's a family connection,' I said. 'Come on, Michael, or we'll miss the train.'

We got out of the house as quickly as possible. It was drizzling so I put on Michael's school sweater. The air felt very cool and fresh. We'd both of us been fibbing about the train. It was only three o'clock and we hadn't planned to go back until five at the earliest, but we walked in the direction of the station nevertheless.

'I wish we hadn't come now,' I said at last.

'You've got your father's address.'

'Isn't it silly, him living quite near me? I can get the train and call any time. Only I don't feel like it now. I don't think he sounds very nice, do you?'

'You can't really go by what that fat old bag said.'

'I hated her, didn't you? She was so horrible to him.'

'Not really horrible. But I know what you mean.'

'Imagine living his life in that stinking room, locked up with her. We should have done something.'

'There's nothing we can do.'

'My father should do something.'

'I shouldn't think the geriatric ward of a hospital would be much better. Probably worse.'

'Why doesn't he look after him himself, for God's sake?'

'You don't know what it's like, caring for a chronic invalid. And it would be his wife that had to do all the dirty work.'

'Michael, that smell. You don't think – well, that he

needed changing or anything? You know what I mean. She wouldn't just leave him lying in it, would she?'

'No, I should think it was just the commode.'

'The what?'

'Didn't you see that chair thing by the bed? The cushion comes off and there's a sort of bucket inside the chair and you go to the loo in it.'

'Ugh.'

'Well, he's too frail and wobbly to balance on a chamber-pot, isn't he? And she can't carry him to the toilet. Whoops. Lavatory.'

I couldn't smile this time. 'You were lovely with him, Michael. I wish I could have talked to him the way you did, and straightened his pillows and everything. I just stood there. I was so useless. And yet I'm the one who's supposed to be related to him,' I said miserably.

'You were frightened of him, that's all. Most people are frightened of invalids and don't know what to do. It's nothing to be ashamed of.'

'But why aren't you frightened?'

'Because I'm used to that sort of thing. My Dad's an invalid.'

I stared at Michael. 'Really?'

'Really. He's got multiple sclerosis. He's had it for years. He's in a wheelchair now.'

'Oh Michael. I'm sorry.'

'Don't be daft. You don't have to talk in that hushed voice.'

'Why didn't you tell me before?'

Michael made a face. 'I don't like talking about him. I don't like him, full stop. And don't look so shocked. Why should I like him just because he's ill? He's a bad tempered, selfish sod who's forever complaining. He never once thanks my mother for all she does for him. And he can't stick me. I'm the world's number one failure as far as he's concerned. He's a big man, and he used to be very strong before the disease developed. He fancied himself as a sportsman although I don't think he was that good. Just the school football and cricket team, that sort of thing. Now he's stuck in a wheelchair, he wants a big thick sporty son to do his living for him. Well, ha ha. I'm the only son he's got. I can't catch a ball, I can't hit a ball. Consequently my father thinks I haven't *got* any balls.'

'Isn't he pleased that you're clever?'

'You're joking! Maybe if I shone at Maths or Science it wouldn't be so bad. But all the Arts subjects? Do you know something, he calls me Mary, not Michael. Mary the Fairy.'

'I wish there weren't any such thing as fathers,' I said. This time I reached out and held Michael's hand. We walked hand in hand to the station. We'd had enough of Chineford so we caught the 3.20 home.

We played paper games for a bit, but I badly wanted to think so I pretended to be sleepy. I spent the last hour of the journey with my eyes closed, going over everything in my head, but I still hadn't got anywhere when Michael gently shook me and told me we were in London. We caught the tube from Paddington to Waterloo. I pulled myself together in the train home and chatted until Michael got off at Blyton Park. I went on to Kingtown and stood on the platform for a full ten minutes, trying to make up my mind.

I'd had a long, tiring day. It was getting even colder. I looked grubby and bedraggled. I knew that the sensible thing to do would be to go home and have a good meal and an early night. I could go to Lychmond tomorrow or the next day. Any day. This year, next year, sometime, never.

No, it was now or never. I crossed to the other side of the platform and caught the next train back to London.

# *Chapter 11*

$T$ HE house was in an exclusive leafy cul-de-sac just off Lychmond Hill. It was tall and white and elegant, with wistaria growing up the walls and beautiful art nouveau stained glass decorations on all the windows. I looked at the red and green swirls and loops and wanted to hurl bricks until they were all shattered. How dare my father live in this palace of a house, tucked away behind his tasteful, olive-green door? What about his father mouldering in that sad, smelly house in Chineford? And what about me?

He could have found me if he'd really tried. It wasn't as if it had been hard for me to find him, it had been ludicrously easy. Yet he hadn't come to see me once, not even when I was a baby. My mother was seventeen years old when she had me. How could he have let her take all the responsibility? He hadn't even tried to help us out financially.

I thought of all the depressing furnished rooms we'd lived in, the nagging neighbours and the scornful landladies, the wood-lice creeping in every corner of the room, the green mould growing on the furniture, even in the folds of the clothes hanging in our plastic wardrobe. We'd lived like that. He'd lived like this.

I wasn't frightened any more. I didn't give a damn if I made things awkward for him. Perhaps it was about time.

The green door had a brass knocker in the shape of a lion's head. I rapped it loudly. The lion grimaced at me. It was so brightly polished I could see a small, distorted image of myself scowling back. The door was flung open almost immediately and a middle-aged man in a dinner suit said hello to me in a bright, welcoming voice, as if he'd been expecting me. But then the smile faded from his face and he looked puzzled.

'Hello?' he repeated uncertainly.

'Are you Mr Pilbeam?'

'I am indeed.'

I was face to face with him at last. My father. We didn't look alike. He was a big man, with a paunch that his well-cut dinner-jacket couldn't quite hide. His face was baby pink and plump. His recently trimmed hair was fairer than mine and his eyes were grey, pale behind his heavy horn-rimmed glasses. He looked a little familiar, but only because I'd seen so many men like him.

'Are you a friend of Caroline's?' he said. 'Can't she manage to baby-sit tonight after all?'

'I don't know. I don't know any Carolines.'

'Sorry. My mistake. Well, how can I help you, dear?'

'I'm not sure. Do you want to help me?'

He glanced at his watch with one impatient flick of his immaculate shirt cuff.

'Look, are you one of these little religious ladies who worship the Maharishi or the Chief Moonie or whatever? If so I rather think we're wasting each other's time. I'm in a bit of a rush to go out at the moment, as you can see, so perhaps we'd better say farewell.'

'You're rather good at saying farewell, aren't you?'

'What on earth do you mean? Are you all right?'

I was shivering in a spectacular fashion because I was so cold and so angry.

'Yes, but no thanks to you.'

'I don't know what you're talking about. I don't know you, do I?'

'You should know me. Didn't it ever occur to you that I might turn up?'

'Look, I'm not very fond of riddles.'

Someone called from upstairs, 'If that's Caroline, darling, will you ask her to be an angel and come and see Vicky in her bath.'

'Come and see me, Caro, I'm all bare,' a child shouted excitedly.

'No, it's not Caroline, not yet,' David Pilbeam called. He turned to me. 'Who are you?'

'I'm your daughter,' I said, and then I gave an awful high-pitched giggle because it sounded so ridiculously melo-dramatic.

I thought he'd go white or perhaps blush. Falter, maybe stagger alarmingly. But he simply looked at me as if I was a lunatic.

'Look dear, you're obviously very distraught,' he said warily, as if I really were deranged. 'I don't know what your problem is or why you've come to me, but I'm afraid I can't help you.'

'You knew my mother, Mary.'

He still looked genuinely blank.

'*Mary*. You went out with her when you were eighteen, in Chineford.'

He stared at me, reacting at last. He pushed his glasses further up his nose and then rubbed the middle of his forehead, as if he were trying to soothe a sudden head-ache.

'Good God,' he said. He looked at me carefully, and I wished I didn't look so bedraggled, although I despised myself for minding what he thought of me. 'Why aren't you wearing a coat? You're shivering,' he said.

'So you believe me now, do you?'

'Who sent you here? Your mother?'

'No!'

'Well how did you know how to find me?'

'I went to Chineford, and the housekeeper lady gave me your address. She's very fed up with you, by the way. She says you ought to find a proper home for your father.'

'What? Look, how does my father come into all this? What do you *want*?'

'I just want to talk to you, that's all.'

He rubbed his forehead again and then looked behind him, into the hall. There were splashing noises and squeals coming from the bathroom upstairs.

'Well – it's – it's a bit difficult now. We're going out and I've got this baby-sitter due any minute. Look, er, Mary –'

'I'm not Mary. That's my mother's name. I'm Sandra,' I said indignantly.

'Well, Sandra, as I expect you realise, this is a bit of a shock for me. I – I didn't even. . . . Well, anyway. We'll have to arrange to meet sometime and then we'll have a proper talk, if that's what you want. Perhaps one lunch-time next week, something like that? And that will give me a chance to mull things over a bit. All right?' He put his hand on the door, about to close it in my face.

'You can't just get rid of me like this. I've travelled hundreds of miles to see you,' I said. Well, I had, if you counted my return journey to Chineford.

'Be reasonable, Sandra. I can hardly ask you in now, can I? Surely you realise my wife and children are upstairs?'

'You haven't told your wife about me?'

'Of course not! And she's not going to be told either, let's get that straight for a start.'

'You can't boss me around and tell me what to do. And you can't stop me telling your wife anyway,' I said defiantly. His hand was still on the door so I added, 'If you shut the door on me I shall just knock again.'

'How old are you?'

'Fifteen. Your mental arithmetic's not very good, is it?'

'You're a cheeky little baggage, aren't you? All right, we'll talk. Now. Only I'm not prepared to carry on this ridiculous furtive conversation on my own doorstep. There's a little café just five minutes away. It's called the Coffeepot. You go down this road and it's on Lychmond hill, on the left as you go down. I'll meet you there as soon as I can get away. Right?'

'You won't come.'

'Yes, I will. I promise. Now off you go, there's a good girl. I'll see you there.'

This time he did shut the door on me. I stood staring at the ugly brass lion, wondering whether to knock again, as I'd threatened, but I didn't quite dare. I trailed away instead, walking along the road and down the hill, obediently making my way to the Coffeepot. I went inside and ordered a coffee and then sat in the window. I kept looking out but I was sure

90

he wouldn't come. It was very warm and steamy in the café but I couldn't stop shivering. I hugged myself, hanging on tightly to my elbows. I couldn't let myself burst into tears, not here.

I still couldn't quite take it in. I'd spoken to my father. I'd stood up to him. But it wasn't going to make any difference. I imagined him telling his wife that some idiot girl had pestered him at the door, but he'd managed to get rid of her. I saw him taking off his black jacket, rolling up his crisp, white shirt-sleeves, and wrapping little Vicky in a towel. He'd tuck her into bed with a special cuddle and kiss, her and her nameless brother or sister, and then he'd go off to his dinner or dance with his wife, leaving Caroline in charge, and he'd never give a second thought to me sitting in this café crying. . . .

'Hello. What's up?'

David Pilbeam sat down at my table. He was wearing a fawn trench coat over his dinner-suit. His glasses steamed up and he wiped them with a carefully ironed handkerchief. There were two shiny pink sores on his nose, where his glasses rubbed. He looked different without his glasses, not so authoritative.

'Are you crying?' He handed me his handkerchief, but I shook my head and wiped my face with the back of my hand.

He ordered a coffee for himself and asked if I wanted anything to eat.

'No thanks.'

'I shan't have anything either. I'm supposed to be starting a five course meal in half an hour.'

'What did you tell your wife?'

'I told her you were Mrs Alcott's daughter. Mrs Alcott is the woman in Chineford who looks after the house for my father.'

'She looks after *him*. You're not the slightest bit concerned about him, are you? It's awful, he can't even talk properly and he just has to lie in bed all day and he's obviously terribly unhappy. Why don't you go and see him?'

'I don't really see that it's any of your business, but I went to see my father less than a month ago. Mrs Alcott enjoys making herself out to be a martyr, but I pay her a considerable sum, and whenever I've raised the question of a nursing home for my father she's always seemed appalled at the idea. Father himself has made it quite clear that he can't bear the idea of going into a home or hospital. I know he gets very down at times but there's very little I can do about it. When my mother died Charmian – my wife – and I begged him to sell the house and make his home with us but he wouldn't hear of it.'

'You've got it all off pat, haven't you? Kidding yourself, so you needn't feel guilty. And how could you tell your wife I'm that horrid woman's daughter!'

'It was the only thing I could think of. Mrs Alcott's daughter has actually come to see me in the past, and she's an incredibly tiresome woman. Whenever Mrs Alcott fancies she has a grievance she phones her daughter in Roehampton, and the wretched daughter lumbers over here – she's even fatter than her mother – and she starts whining.'

'And now you've got another daughter whining on your doorstep. Your own daughter this time.'

'Now hang on. You aren't necessarily *my* daughter at all.'

'What do you mean?'

'I didn't really know your mother very well. We only went out together a handful of times.'

'So you're saying my mother's lying, are you?'

'Now simmer down. I'm not saying anything of the sort. I'm simply saying that you can't necessarily prove that we're related.'

'You're acting as if I'm trying to blackmail you or something.'

'Well, it did cross my mind.'

'Do you really think I got in touch with you to blackmail you?' I said, appalled.

'No, all right. I'm sorry. But why did you? Why did you get in touch with me?'

I looked down at the table, running my finger along the patterned edge of the plastic cloth. I didn't know what to say. There were so many reasons and yet I couldn't say any of them, not to him.

'I don't know. I suppose I just wanted to see what you're like. Didn't you ever wonder about me? Why didn't you ever come to see me?'

'I didn't even know your mother had had a baby.'

'You liar! She told you she was pregnant in a café somewhere, just like this one, and you cried.'

'All right, there's no need to shout. Yes, she told me, and yes, I very upset. But after that – well, we didn't really see much of each other.'

'Yes, you ditched her.'

'Not exactly. I went away to university.'

'Very convenient. You could at least have written to her.'

'I did write.'

'Once.'

'How do you know that?'

'Because my mother kept your letter.'

'Did she?' He had the nerve to look pleased.

'Just for a bit. Then she tore it up, but she told me all about it. What happened to your book? Did it ever get published?'

'What book?'

'You were writing a book. You read some of it to my mother.'

'Did I? Oh, wait a minute. Yes, I remember. I wonder what ever happened to it?'

'So you didn't finish it.'

'No.'

'And you're not a novelist now?'

'Good God, no. What gave you that idea? No, I'm in advertising, actually. Well, that's writing of a sort, isn't it, although nowadays I don't have much to do with the creative side, more's the pity.'

'Advertising,' I said scornfully. 'That's why you're so good at telling lies.'

'What lies am I telling you, Sandra?'

'Well, not lies then, but you're being so evasive. I thought when we actually met at last we'd *talk* to each other. Not like this. All my life I've been wondering about you, trying to imagine what you're like, and yet you seem to have forgotten all about me.'

'I told you, I didn't even know that your mother had actually had a baby. For all I knew she might have – well. . . .'

'You knew she wouldn't ever have had an abortion! She wouldn't have known how to go about it and she wouldn't have had the money anyway. Didn't you even find out if I was a boy or a girl? Didn't you ever wonder?'

'I don't know. It's so long ago. And I was in my first year at university. It was a completely different world for me, don't forget. I suppose I did think about your mother and I felt rotten about it, but it wasn't as if we'd had a passionate love affair. We met at a party and drifted together for a few weeks, that's all.'

'She loved you. That's why she slept with you. She thought you were wonderful. Only you walked out of her life and left her literally holding the baby.'

'Yes, all right, you've made your point. I'm not very proud of the way I behaved. But there's not much I can do about it now.'

'My grandparents threw my mother out. She had to do some awful jobs and she had a breakdown when I was five. I had to go into Care.'

He really did look shocked at that. 'I had no idea. How are things now? Your mother recovered?'

'No thanks to you.'

'What about your financial situation? Perhaps there's some way I could help?'

'We don't want your filthy money, thanks. My mother's fine now. She's married, and she's got another child and she's very happy.'

'Good. Well. That's a relief.' He sipped coffee and glanced at his watch.

'You can't wait to get away, can you? All right then, go. I wouldn't want to make you miss one of your five dinner courses.'

'Look, give me your address and telephone number. Write it here for me.' He handed me his diary.

I wrote and he looked disconcerted when he read my address.

'So you don't live that far away. Perhaps we could see each other from time to time. You're fifteen, you say? Starting your O-level year at school? What do you like best?'

'English.'

'Ah! And what do you want to do? Do *you* want to be a writer?'

'Not really,' I lied.

'Oh well, there's plenty of time for you to make up your mind.' He looked at his watch again. 'Well, I really have to go now, Sandra. But tell you what. Here's my work phone number. Give me a ring there rather than at home. Any time you feel like it, all right? Now, how are you going to get home? Can I give you a lift anywhere?'

'No, I've got a return train ticket.'

'Right. Well. I don't quite know what to say. I'm sorry. I suppose you've every right to feel bitter. Well. Goodbye then. Look after yourself. You've got my work number safe, haven't you? Right. Goodbye.'

I waited until he'd gone and then I tore the piece of paper with his phone number into tiny shreds and scattered them under my chair.

# *Chapter 12*

*I* hadn't seriously expected it to be like my story, with my father hugging me and telling me that he'd been longing for this moment all my life. But I had expected our meeting to be meaningful. I'd given my father a nasty shock – but that was all. He'd wept nearly sixteen years ago when he knew I was on the way, but I couldn't imagine that sleek self-satisfied man crying now. How could my mother ever have thought him wonderful?

I tried to imagine them meeting at this party, talking, dancing together, maybe making love that very first time. Did it happen on a bed, amongst a pile of other people's coats, or outside in the back of someone's car, or up against a wall in a chilly moonlit garden? What did they call each other? Did he keep his glasses on? Did they take their clothes off or fumble fully dressed? David Pilbeam, having it off at last with a dim little girl who'd probably had too many Babychams. Silly Mary, kidding herself she was in love because a posh boy kissed her and told her she was beautiful. How many times did they actually go out together? Five times, ten at the most? And when was I conceived?

It was weird to think that if either of them had been more experienced I wouldn't exist. I *hadn't* existed for my father. He'd admitted it. He hadn't given me a first thought, let alone a second. And he hadn't given me much thought now, when he knew I was flesh and blood, *his* flesh and blood. He'd asked me if I was doing O-levels and what I wanted to do when I left school, like a polite stranger. That's all he was, a stranger who just happened (because my mother had one drink too many? Because he hadn't had the nerve to buy a packet of Durex? Because it was the wrong time of the month? Because quite by chance they were both asked to the same wretched party?) to have fathered me.

I cried in the café and I cried on the train home to Kingtown, but I wasn't crying because my father didn't care about me. I was crying because I couldn't care about him. I'd been so sure that there would be an instinctive closeness between us. But it wasn't like that at all. I couldn't fling my arms round him and call him Dad. I couldn't touch him any more than I could touch his poor sick father. I'd discovered a whole new family – and yet *another* cutie pie half-sister – but I didn't belong there either. Even if I'd always lived with them and been a Pilbeam I'd still not belong.

It was late when I got back home at last and I expected a row. I got one too.

'You could have bloody phoned,' Stan kept saying, when I lied and told them I'd gone to Michael's for supper after we'd got back from the coast. 'Your Mum's been worried sick. We expected you back hours ago.'

I was so tired and hungry and cold and fed up that I started crying again, really bawling as if I was Julie's age. Stan blustered on for a bit, but Mum was quite nice. Very nice. She put her arms round me and huddled me against her on the sofa in front of the fire and ran her fingers through my hair, letting me cry smudges down the front of her white nylon polo-neck. Julie had been put to bed but she woke up and came trotting down to see what was going on, and we ended up having buttered toast and cups of cocoa, all four of us. Then I remembered my rock and I handed them each a pink stick.

It wasn't until the next afternoon that Mum looked carefully at her half-finished stick of rock and read the little crimson letters. CHINEFORD.

'I thought you said you and Michael had gone to Brighton?' she said.

I'd made up a lovely day for us. We'd wandered round the Lanes and gone round the Pavilion and the museum and then had a long walk along the cliffs in spite of the rain.

97

I couldn't think of any way to get out of it. They'd hardly be selling sticks of Chineford rock in Brighton.

'You went all the way to Chineford yesterday?' she said.

'Yes.'

'But you said – you mean that story about Brighton was just a whole load of lies?' She sounded more worried than angry.

'Yes. I didn't want you to know that I'd been to Chineford.'

'What did you go there for?' she asked, nibbling at a shred of loose skin on her lip. It made her look ugly and childish and I suddenly loved her.

'It was a silly idea.'

'I suppose you went to look for your father.'

'I just wanted to see what the place was like. I didn't think much of it. And the rain didn't help.'

'It's a wonder you didn't catch your death of cold. I told you to wear your jacket and a sensible woollie.' She paused. 'Did you – you didn't . . . ?'

'Find him? No, of course not. And I don't really want to either,' I said firmly.

'Oh well. It's up to you, I suppose,' Mum said awkwardly. She thought for a moment. 'You aren't half a convincing little liar. No wonder you're so good at story writing.'

I lied to Michael too. When I met him on Monday morning he asked me if I wanted to go to Lychmond to find my father's house.

'No, I don't think there's much point,' I said. 'This whole thing's become farcical. Why should I want to meet him? I mean, what's the point? We're hardly likely to spot each other in the rosy distance and run together in slow motion and fall into each other's arms, like lovers in a television commercial.'

'You've changed your tune. You're willing to spend a fortune on train fares all the way to Chineford but you can't be bothered to nip across London to Lychmond.'

'It's not that I can't be bothered, I just don't want to any more. Do stop going on about it, Michael. Come on, let's do something. Let's go on the common and do some Michaelandra. It's our last chance. Mum says I've got to go round the town with her tomorrow getting my plimsolls and a new Science overall and other school rubbish, then on Wednesday Stan's got the day off and she wants us all to go out to the Zoo or the seaside or somewhere, and then school starts on Thursday.'

Mum had invited Michael too. I'd quickly made up some excuse and Stan had raised his eyebrows sceptically.

'Don't give us that waffle, Sandra,' he'd said. 'You just don't want your snobby boy-friend to meet your family, that's what it is. You're ashamed of us, aren't you?'

But on Monday I found out I was ashamed of Michael. As soon as we'd found a secluded spot on the common and got all our books and pencils and felt tips out it started raining again. We bundled everything away and sheltered under the trees for a while, but the rain stayed steady and relentless.

'We can always go to the library,' Michael said, but when we got to the reference library it was full of schoolchildren arguing in whispers and muttering men in dank raincoats, and we couldn't possibly make up Michaelandra in front of them. We packed up all our things yet again and went and had a milk shake in a Wimpy.

We managed to get a table for two right in the corner at the back, and wondered if we might be able to work there if we ordered something to eat or drink every twenty minutes or so. I still had some of my story money left and Michael certainly still had his enormous appetite. But as soon as we started getting the exercise books out the waitress came up shaking her head.

'You can put that lot right away. I'm not having you kids doing your homework in here. This isn't the place for that at all. You just finish up your drinks and then clear off somewhere else. This is a café, not a school.'

We wandered disconsolately round the town, wet and fed up. There were all sorts of places where we could go to do something specific, like eat or skate or swim or watch a film, but nowhere where we could just sit and do what we wanted.

I started fantasising about the attic flat I was going to live in when I left school and I quite fancied the idea of wandering round the town looking for sofas and cushions and things for furniture, but although Michael liked most pretend games this one bored him silly. So we went to Mallington Museum, but we'd been there so many times already that summer that the glass cages of faded birds and the Roman arrowheads seemed achingly boring.

We went and had an early lunch, after a stupid argument. I said that as I was paying I ought to be the one to decide where we ate and I wanted to go to the health food restaurant in Kingtown. Michael said that no one but a gullible fool would willingly pay 46 pence for a glass of flat apple juice and 55 pence for a stodgy cardboard flavoured vegetable turnover, and if the food was so healthy why did that drippy bloke with the beard who served it have such terrible pimples on his face?

Michael voted for a hamburger and chips and another milk shake. That should have been fine with me. I'd wanted Monday to be special to make up for the difficult day at Chineford. I'd planned to take Michael for a really huge junky meal, after we'd had a satisfying session making up Michaelandra. I was even going to treat him to a Knicker Bocker Glory after his hamburger, but now I argued senselessly that I couldn't afford that sort of meal and we ended up in a dreary sandwich bar, silently munching damp egg sandwiches.

'Thank you so much for my delicious, nourishing meal,' Michael said nastily. 'Your generosity overwhelms me, Sandra.'

'Well, it's ridiculous, me for ever being the one who forks out for everything,' I snapped, as we went outside. 'This isn't liberation, it's exploitation. You take it for granted now that I'm the twit who doles out the money.'

I knew it wasn't true at all. Michael tried very hard to pay his way whenever he could. He looked white and pinched and I hated myself. I hoped he'd snub me with a really caustic reply but he didn't say anything, and I felt even worse.

'I'm sorry,' I said hopelessly. 'I don't know what's the matter with me, Michael. I really am sorry.'

'It's all right,' Michael muttered, but it obviously wasn't.

We walked in silence through the rain. I was wearing my jacket this time, and I had sensible sandals, but the soggy cuffs of my dungarees flapped uncomfortably against my legs.

'What shall we do?' I asked. What I really wanted to do was to go home, have a hot bath and a hot drink, and then curl up in my dressing-gown with a good book. But it was our last day together and so I tried to make an effort.

'It's a bit silly, just wandering round getting wetter and wetter. Let's go to the pictures, eh?'

'You can, if you want,' said Michael.

'Don't you want to?'

'I haven't got any money, have I?'

'Oh Michael! Don't be like that. I've said I'm sorry. What else can I do? Come on, let's go and see what's on at the Granada.'

I nearly had to go down on my knees and beg before he'd give in. There was a sexy X film and a kids' cartoon thing and a romantic American film that I'd already seen.

'But it's quite good, really. Let's go and see that.'

'I've seen it too. There's more intellectual content in the Walt Disney,' said Michael. 'Still, it's your money so you get to choose.'

'Do you have to be so childish? Okay, we'll go to the cartoon, if that's the sort of thing that turns you on.'

There was a queue for all the films so we went and stood in it to continue our argument.

'Hey look, it's Sandra!'

I turned round, my heart thudding. Kim and Debra were standing in the queue just in front of us. They both wore very tight skirts and high heels and elaborate make-up. Debra had a green streak in the front of her hair and green nail varnish to match. She waved her hand, fanning her ghoulish nails affectedly. She looked me up and down and then she looked at Michael. My stomach started churning. He was wearing his awful red sweater and his mother had recently cut his hair. He looked about eleven years old.

'Is that your brother?' said Debra.

Kim knew I didn't have a brother.

'Is he your boy-friend, San?' Kim said, her eyes sparkling. 'Do introduce us, eh?'

'Shut up,' I mumbled, wanting to die. I saw Kim and Debra exchange glances. It would be all round our year on Thursday. They'd never stop teasing me. I could hear it already. 'Hey, San, do you change your boy-friend's nappies before you go out?' 'Do tell me where your boy-friend gets his haircut, it's ever so trendy.' 'What's your boy-friend's favourite telly programme, "Andy Pandy"?'

'I'm Michael Westaway,' Michael said.

It's a perfectly ordinary name and he said it in a perfectly ordinary manner, but Debra and Kim nudged each other and collapsed into helpless giggles. I found I had a stupid grin on my face too although I've never felt less like laughing in my life.

'Get him!' Debra spluttered.

'How long have you and San been going out then?' said Kim.

'We're not *going* out,' I said. 'Do shut up, you two.'

'Ooh, hoity toity,' said Debra. 'What film are you going to see then? Are you two going to hold hands in the back row, eh? Naughty!'

'Who *is* he, San?' Kim said, coming up close and whispering in my ear. 'Is he your boy-friend?'

'Of course not. He's just some kid I know. I can't stick him.' I whispered it, but Michael looked at me and I knew he'd heard. I waited, frozen. Michael shrugged his shoulders and walked off. I didn't follow him. I didn't even call after him. I stood in the queue with Kim and Debra and we went to see the American film together, the three of us.

Kim and Debra kept whispering to each other in the cinema. I stared straight ahead, my eyes stinging, not seeing the film at all. All I could see was a small pale boy with glasses and sticking out hair and an awful red sweater and a plastic airline bag. Half-way through the film I pretended I had to go to the Ladies and pushed past Kim and Debra. I went straight out of the exit. I had this mad idea that Michael might be standing outside the cinema waiting for me, but of course he wasn't.

So I went home and I had my hot drink and then I had my hot bath. I sat crying in my bath for a very long time. I seemed to have done a great deal of crying throughout the summer. It hadn't really got me anywhere. I thought about David Pilbeam crying in the café when he knew I was on the way. Perhaps he hadn't been sorry for my mother, perhaps he'd just been sorry for himself. I got out of the bath. My skin was shrivelled and I was salmon pink all over. I wiped the steam off the bathroom cabinet mirror with my towel and stared at myself. I looked hideous, with my hair scraped up into a bun to stop it getting wet, my eyes red and puffy from crying and two spots on my nose and one on my chin. Who the hell did I think I was, expecting everybody else to be perfect?

I dried myself and got dressed in my shirt and denim skirt. Mum had hung up my dungarees and had stuffed my sandals with newspaper.

'Feeling better, love?' she said brightly. She had obviously heard me crying in my bath.

'A bit,' I said. 'Mum, I've had a silly row with Michael. I want to try and find his phone number. If we make it up, can I ask him out with us on Wednesday?'

'Well, yes. I suppose so. Yes, of course, lovie. Oh dear, perhaps we'd better go somewhere more exciting than the zoo. He's a bit grand for that, isn't he?'

'Oh Mum, I want to go to see the monkeys and the elephants, you promised!' Julie wailed.

'We'll still go to the zoo.' I took a deep breath. 'Mum, about Michael . . . I sort of exaggerated a bit.'

'How do you mean, love?'

'I – well – he's only fourteen. Nearly fourteen, anyway. And he's as small as me. He isn't rich either. They're quite poor actually, because his father's an invalid. And he's not very good-looking at all.'

'Oh Sandra!' Mum looked bewildered. 'Whatever made you say all that then?'

'I don't know, I was just daft. Can I phone him now and ask him?'

'Yes, of course.'

There were three Westaways in Blyton Park. It was third time lucky. Michael's mother answered.

'Is that Mrs Westaway? Do you have a son called Michael? Oh good. Is he there, please? It's a friend of his. Sandra.'

She put the phone down. I could hear her talking to someone. I waited, huddled up over the phone, wondering what I was going to do if he wouldn't talk to me.

'Hello?'

I let out my breath. 'Michael? It's me.'

'So I gathered.'

'Michael, I'm sorry. I didn't mean that. I don't know why I was such an idiot. I don't even like those girls. I was hateful to you today. I keep on being hateful to you, but I don't mean it, really I don't. Michael, will you still be friends with me?'

'Of course I will, twit. How did you know my telephone number?'

'How do you think? I looked you up in the directory.'

'You aren't half lucky all the men in your life have got distinctive names. What would you have done if I was Michael Smith?'

'"I'd have ploughed through the thousands of Smiths in the phone book," Sexy Sandra said fervently, because she'd come to her senses at last and realised that her only chance of true happiness lay with lovelorn Mike,' I said, and we both laughed.

The laugh was actually on me, because when that teenage magazine eventually got round to publishing my story they'd left out all my poetic bits and the descriptive passages and most of the interesting conversation. I didn't think much of what was left. It didn't seem like my story at all. They'd even changed the heroine's name. She wasn't Rosamund any more. They'd called her Sandra!

# *Afterword*

---

'Is it true?'

'Are you Sandra?'

'Did you try to find your real father?'

That's what people ask. And I always feel awful having to say that it's not true at all. I made it all up. I'm not Sandra. I didn't lead her sort of life. The whole story is a pack of lies from start to finish. That's what fiction is. Lies. It even says so in the dictionary: 'Literary works invented by the imagination; an invented story or explanation; lie.'

So why did I invent my story? What sort of an explanation is it? Why lie?

The one thing I have in common with Sandra is that I've always wanted to be a writer ever since I was little. I was always making up stories in my head too. I didn't even think of them as stories at first. It was just my weird way of playing.

Did you ever have imaginary friends when you were younger? I started off with Gwenny when I was about two. She was a little girl who looked just like me and wore the same clothes and lived in the same flat but she was always naughty whereas I was always good. So when an ornament got broken or a chocolate biscuit disappeared I could always say that it wasn't *me*, it was Gwenny. Gwenny and I had a lot of fun together.

Then when I was about four or five I started on King. Sometimes I was King. Sometimes I was his Queen, or one of the Princesses. Sometimes I was several of King's loyal subjects. I was even King's Deadly Enemy *and* the Deadly Enemy's Army. I used to curl up in bed at night or lock myself in the bathroom during the day and commune with King and country. My parents once heard me muttering away and put their ears to the door and listened and when I eventually emerged they were absolutely doubled up with laughter.

I didn't find it funny at all then. I learnt to do my making up silently, inside my head—and when I got a bit older and could print words quickly enough I wrote some of my stories in special exercise books from Woolworths with shiny red covers.

I was still scribbling in those notebooks when I was fifteen like Sandra. I wanted to write books for my own age group. There weren't that many around then. There was a special shelf for teenagers in my library but it mostly contained extraordinary career stories with titles like *Donald is a Dentist* and *Vera is a Vet*. I couldn't get excited about Donald and Vera and their respective careers. They weren't a bit like me or my friends. Donald might peer into a girl's mouth to inspect her fillings but he never tried to kiss anyone. Vera might fondle a poorly poodle but she didn't ever cuddle up with a boy.

There was a lot of kissing and cuddling going on in the teenage magazines I read but somehow that world didn't seem very convincing either. I wanted to read about the agony of going to a disco and getting ignored by all the boys (girls didn't dare ask boys to dance in those days). I wanted to read about spots and how you want to go around with a paper bag over your head when you've got this great hideous pustule erupting on the end of your nose. I wanted to read about the torture of a first date and how neither of you knows what to say and there are these terrible silences. I wanted to read about the loneliness when your best friend suddenly goes off with someone else and you haven't got anyone to go round with. I wanted to read about the rows you have with your parents who can't ever seem to understand what it's like to be young. I wanted to read about the disappointment of going out with a fantastic boy you've been fancying for ages only to find out he's deadly boring and just wants to show off about himself, and he's got sweaty hands and his after-shave smells like lavatory cleaner.

But the magazine stories described a fairy tale world where everyone gets dances at discos, and spots disappear over night—so long as you use the right magic ointment, and every single romance ends happily ever after with a long passionate kiss.

So I kept trying to write the sort of story I wanted to read. I didn't want to write *my* story though. I couldn't think of anything more boring than writing out a long account of my own life. It was much more fun to make things up. To invent (King and country). To lie (It wasn't me, it was Gwenny). But of course by this time I'd grown out of Gwennys and Kings and Queens. I wanted to write about much more realistic imaginary people—girls and boys so real you believed you might actually bump into them.

I wrote other things when I was older but I kept thinking about that book for teenagers. And then one day I'd been reading about adopted children trying to trace their real mothers and I wondered how it would feel not to have any idea what your mother was like. Or father, for that matter. And Sandra suddenly started up in my head. You see I still have imaginary friends. Only now I'm a writer I get to call them characters for my new books.

It was strange rereading *Nobody's Perfect* when I was asked to write this afterword. The book certainly isn't perfect! I kept wanting to change bits. And it's got stuck in a little time warp. Poor Sandra cares a lot about the way she looks and yet she has to wear the most dreadfully out of date clothes because the book was written a few years ago. If you care about clothes too then how about taking Sandra on an imaginary trip to *Miss Selfridge* to get her some decent new clothes?

It's funny when your own imaginary characters get published in a proper book. I like the cover illustrations for the hardback and the paperback of *Nobody's Perfect* but the girl and boy aren't quite the way I'd imagined Sandra and Michael. How could they be? The artist can't see into my own head. It was even odder when a little extract from the book was on a school television programme. The children playing the parts did it so marvellously but it somehow made me feel Sandra and Michael weren't quite mine any more.

I wonder what you thought of Sandra? And Michael too. I'd have given anything for a friend like Michael. Well, I would now. Maybe I'd have been stupid enough to find him a bit of an embarrassment when I was Sandra's age. I sometimes wonder whether they stayed best friends. Do you want to know something really odd? Maybe I've started to believe my own stories, inventions, lies. Every time I go to the British Museum I can't help hoping I might just bump into Sandra and Michael.

JACQUELINE WILSON

## Archway Novels

| | |
|---|---|
| **The Poacher's Son**   by Rachel Anderson | 0 19 271545 3 |
| **Friend Fire and the Dark Wings**   by J G Fyson | 0 19 271539 9 |
| **Terry on the Fence**   by Bernard Ashley | 0 19 271537 2 |
| **The Oak and the Ash**   by Frederick Grice | 0 19 271538 0 |
| **Break in the Sun**   by Bernard Ashley | 0 19 271476 7 |
| **Revolt at Ratcliffe's Rags**   by Gillian Cross | 0 19 271477 5 |
| **Fox Farm**   by Eileen Dunlop | 0 19 271478 3 |
| **Collision Course**   by Nigel Hinton | 0 19 271479 1 |
| **A Pattern of Roses**   by K M Peyton | 0 19 271499 6 |
| **The Bonny Pit Laddie**   by Frederick Grice | 0 19 271498 8 |
| **A Midsummer Night's Death**   by K M Peyton | 0 19 271480 5 |
| **Moses Beech**   by Ian Strachan | 0 19 271481 3 |
| **Frontier Wolf**   by Rosemary Sutcliff | 0 19 271482 1 |
| **The Islanders**   by John Rowe Townsend | 0 19 271483 X |
| **The Dark Behind the Curtain**   by Gillian Cross | 0 19 271500 3 |
| **The Black Lamp**   by Peter Carter | 0 19 271497 X |
| **The Demon Headmaster**   by Gillian Cross | 0 19 271553 4 |
| **Brother in the Land**   by Robert Swindells | 0 19 271552 6 |
| **Madatan**   by Peter Carter | 0 19 271577 1 |
| **Nobody's Perfect**   by Jacqueline Wilson | 0 19 271576 3 |
| **The Fat Girl**   by Marilyn Sachs | 0 19 271575 5 |
| **Biker**   by Jon Hardy | 0 19 271579 8 |